Praise for Cara Bastone's romance novels!

'Cara Bastone is one of the m
genre today. With her sig
and honesty, Cara's b
best stories begin
Lyssa Ka

'Cara Bastone handles grief with ... touch, reminding us that life goes o... never dies. This story is tucked inside my heart for good'
Jessica Joyce, *USA Today* bestselling author

'Flawlessly crafted and deeply emotional, *Promise Me Sunshine* grabbed hold of my heart from the very first page and didn't let go. I was laughing, sobbing, and everything in between. The story left me breathless and stayed with me long after I reached The End'
Amy Ewing, *New York Times* bestselling author

'Bastone delivers on this truly heartwarming, funny, and real story. Come for the dog bar, stay for the special, slow-burn romcom'
Abby Jimenez, *New York Times* bestselling author

'*Ready or Not* is the very definition of the perfect slow burn, friends-to-lovers romance. Cara Bastone's voice is wholly unique and sparkles with effervescence and joy. I savored every page'
KJ Dell'Antonia, *New York Times* bestselling author

'An absolute treasure of a book! Cara Bastone gives readers a gift, and pays humanity a compliment, with this warmly witty, profoundly tender story of a love that makes the world bigger and better. One of the most emotionally satisfying romances I've read in years'
Joanna Lowell

'A wholehearted meditation on all kinds of love, this novel is pure joy'
Annabel Monaghan

'With loads of humor, lovable characters, and a first kiss that will leave you flushed and breathless, *Ready or Not* is a delightfully romantic story that celebrates modern love and the excitement of the unexpected. Readers will adore Cara Bastone's joyful, swoony novel!'
Amy Poeppel

Cara Bastone is a full-time writer who lives and writes in Brooklyn with her husband, son and an almost-golden doodle. Her goal with her work is to find the swoon in ordinary love stories. She's been a fan of the romance genre since she found a grocery bag filled with her grandmother's old Harlequin Romance books when she was in high school. She's a fangirl for pretzel sticks, long walks through Prospect Park, and love stories featuring men who aren't hobbled by their own masculinity.

To find out more, visit **carabastone.com** or follow Cara on Instagram **@carabastone**.

By Cara Bastone

Ready or Not
Promise Me Sunshine

Love Lines Series
Call Me Maybe
Sweet Talk
Seatmate

Sweet Talk

CARA BASTONE

HEADLINE
ETERNAL

Originally published in 2021 as an audiobook by Audible Originals
First Published in 2021 by Headline Eternal
An imprint of Headline Publishing Group Limited

This paperback edition published in 2025 by Headline Eternal
An imprint of Headline Publishing Group Limited

3

Cataloguing in Publication Data is available from the British Library

ISBN 978 1 4722 8783 0

Typeset in 11/14 pt Minion Pro by Jouve (UK), Milton Keynes

Printed and bound in Great Britain by Clays Ltd, Elcograf S.p.A.

MIX
Paper | Supporting responsible forestry
FSC® C104740
FSC www.fsc.org

Headline's policy is to use papers that are natural, renewable and recyclable products and made from wood grown in well-managed forests and other controlled sources. The logging and manufacturing processes are expected to conform to the environmental regulations of the country of origin.

HEADLINE PUBLISHING GROUP LIMITED
An Hachette UK Company
Carmelite House
50 Victoria Embankment
London EC4Y 0DZ

The authorised representative in the EEA is Hachette Ireland,
8 Castlecourt Centre, Dublin 15, D15 XTP3, Ireland (email: info@hbgi.ie)

www.headlineeternal.com
www.headline.co.uk
www.hachette.co.uk

For everybody with tool belts.
(Literal ones and emotional ones.)
If you work hard to fix problems, this book is for you.

Chapter One

Jessie

"*Hey, you still up?*"

I nearly choke to death on the humongous bite of dry chocolate cake in my mouth. It's almost 2 a.m., I'm sitting cross-legged on the kitchen counter in my dad's apartment, and I'm pretty sure I just got drunk-texted by the man I have a debilitating crush on.

Only, that wasn't just a text. That was a voice message he texted me. I was not expecting to suddenly hear that movie-star voice in the middle of the night, in the middle of this shoebox kitchen, in the middle of a slice of bad cake that will seriously not budge an inch down my throat. I try to swallow the bite again, and when it still doesn't give up the ghost, I spear my fork into the center of the cake slice for safekeeping and lean over to drink straight from the faucet.

Water runs down my chin, over my ear, and into my hair, and I'm a soggy, gasping mess by the time I give my phone my full attention again. I play the voice message that was just texted to me one more time.

"*Hey, you still up?*"

This has to be a mistake, right? He's never texted or called me before. Not even during daylight hours. I glance at the clock on the screen of the ancient microwave and even though it's missing most of its pixels I still confirm that it is, in fact, the middle of the night. It's officially booty o'clock and he definitely just *you up?*ed me.

The question is whether or not he knows who it is he just propositioned. This has to be a misdial?

So, where do I go from here? Pretend I didn't get it and leave him to discover his mistake on his own? That's probably best . . . but . . . the thing is . . . this guy is so cute. Like, *stupid* cute. And cute isn't even usually my bag. But he's got this big, handsome puppy thing going on that just really . . . makes me wanna . . . Look, there's no way I'm not texting him back.

I'm sure this was a mistake on his end, but that doesn't mean it's not an opportunity on my end and it's the middle of the night, and I just wanna talk to him.

I text back Yeah? with a question mark.

It's kind of brilliant if you think about it.

A moment later another voice message pops up and his voice fills the kitchen again.

"*I didn't wake you up, did I?*"

No, I text back. I was just eating chocolate cake.

I get another incoming voice message almost immediately. "*Chocolate cake? At 2 a.m.? Weirdo.*"

I laugh and text him back.

What did you expect?

"*At 2 a.m.? That you'd either be sleeping and we'd just talk in the morning, or that you'd be racing to meet a shipping deadline,*" he responds.

Who is this person that he thinks he's texting? The middle of the night "you up?" text immediately points toward someone he wants to hook up with. But nothing else has been especially flirty. Not even his tone. In fact, I don't think he's drunk.

No work tonight, I text. Just cake.

"*Ugh. Why are you making me read at this time of night?*"

I blink and listen to that voice message one more time. He doesn't like reading texts? I guess that explains why he's voice-messaging me. I type a few replies, but I delete each one. Because each one is a lie or evasion, and that's not really my style. Instead I press down on the voice-record button. No way out but the truth.

"Because I figured once you heard my voice, you'd realize that you were texting the wrong person." *Whoosh*, I send the message.

I get another voice message almost immediately.

"*Oh, my God. I'm so sorry. I texted the wrong person.*"

"Yup. I figured. Have a good night."

I send that last voice message with a sigh. Well, that was fun while it lasted. Four minutes of tepid texting with a guy who has me confused with someone else has unfortunately been the highlight of my month.

The sad thing is that not only do I want to talk to him, I really just wanna talk to *anybody*. Before that voice message, it had been almost twelve hours since I spoke a word aloud, and that was a simple "thank you" to Miss Laura in 5C when she dropped off the chocolate cake that almost took my life a few minutes ago. With Pops in the care facility, I'm alone almost all the time. Well, except for work, but that doesn't count. My general demeanor doesn't exactly foster small talk, and I don't know anyone well enough for them to actually check in on me.

I hop down and dump the rest of the cake in the trash, because if I don't, I'll just keep eating it, and it tastes like a sponge someone used to wipe up some cocoa powder. I think she forgot the sugar.

I'm sudsing up the plate when my phone dings from the counter. I blink.

Did he text again? But I just *have a good night*ed him. I let him off the hook. There's no reason for him to keep texting after that. I wipe my soapy hands on my sweats and pick up my phone.

"*Okay, this is humiliating. But . . . would you mind telling me who you are?*"

I gape at the phone for a second before jamming my finger on the voice-record button. I assumed he would have looked at the contact information and at least figured out who I was from that. Did he not save my last name or something?

"You still don't know who I am? Then how am I saved in your phone?" I send the message.

A thought occurs to me, and I inwardly cringe. What if he *did* save my last name and that's not the problem? The problem is that even with a first and last name he has no memory of who I am. This is . . . disheartening. Here, I've spent the last two months daydreaming about his dimples, and he can't even put my face to my name. Ouch.

"*I accidentally saved your contact as a bunch of mixed-up letters. I guess I wasn't looking when I was typing it in. You're right next to the person I meant to text in my contact list,*" he messages.

Okay, so not quite as bad as I thought? I think back to the night he got my number from me. It actually makes sense that he would've mistyped in those circumstances. It was a pretty crazy night. He definitely wasn't in his right mind. I guess I can forgive him this.

And now that I'm mulling it over, if he knew who I was, then we would have to stop texting because this would just be super awkward. But as it is, he has no idea who I am. So, I guess I can reply?

"Wow," I send. And just like that he's replying. "*Okay, yes, I definitely deserve that judgmental wow. Like I said, this is majorly humiliating. I . . . take it that you know who I am?*"

"Yes, Eliot Hoffman, I know who you are. I saved your name in my phone properly," I send.

"*Okay . . . I deserve that, too,*" he replies. "*All right, let me think. I recognize your voice, but I can't place it. But I'm saved in your phone by both first and last name, right? Which I'm guessing means that we've met a few times but don't know each other that well.*"

I stare at my phone again for a long second. That assessment is scarily accurate. But that's not the reason my heart has banged its way up into my throat. Is . . . is Eliot Hoffman *chatting* with me right now? I *have a good night*ed him at two in the morning, yet here he is, continuing to text me. I nearly take my thumbnail off in one nervous bite.

I thought the name of the game was going to be how to get out of this conversation with my pride still intact. But no. The name of the game is now chatting with a cute guy in the middle of the night without being the one to accidentally end the conversation first.

Let's see . . . how to explain my overthinking. Ah. Okay. I'm not exactly known for my gentle touch with anything, but especially with guys. I'm one of those girls who punches the guy she likes too hard in the shoulder. If I think someone is cute, I don't blush or bite my lip. I roll my eyes and mildly insult him.

But chatting with Eliot Hoffman right now is like realizing there's some mythical creature standing in my kitchen next to me. If I freak out and rush him, he's going to skitter away, gone for ever, no one would even believe he'd been there in the first place. This is a delicate dance. I clear my throat and think of how to reply.

"Ding ding ding. You get ten points," I send.

He replies immediately, and my blood pressure skyrockets. I probably look like a weightlifter right now. Veins bulging, eyeballs bugging.

"*I get points for this? I can't believe you haven't subtracted a million points for not knowing who you are. You're a generous and forgiving soul.*"

"Good point," I message. "Minus ten points for not knowing who I am. You're back to zero."

He messages back right away. "*Ha! I shouldn't have said anything. Shot myself in the foot. How many points do I get if I outright guess who you are?*"

"How many of these fictional points that mean nothing and literally exist only in our brains?" I respond.

"*Yes, exactly. Those points.*"

"Umm. Two hundred."

"*Okay, deal. If I guess who you are outright, I get two hundred points. But also, if I build up to two hundred points with good guesses, then you just have to tell me.*"

"Considering the fact that you're currently at zero, I'm not concerned. So, deal."

"*Fair warning, though. I'm very competitive.*"

"So let's hear a guess, then."

"*Laura Hepburn?*"

I am instantly and completely consumed with hatred for Laura Hepburn. Whoever she is, I hope that she, um . . . what are the worst things that could happen to a person? Ah! I hope she has a lifetime of sneeze tickles that never actually turn into a sneeze.

"Minus twenty," I message.

I would make it minus a million if I didn't think it would scare him off.

"What?! Minus twenty for wrong guesses? That's way harsh, Tai."

Either he's bored, or secretly he's just as lonely as I am, because he just quoted *Clueless* to a near-stranger that he has absolutely no obligation to be talking to. Why isn't he sleeping right now? Why did he reach out in the middle of the night to whoever he thought I was at the beginning of this conversation? Why does he seem to be just as down to chitchat as I am?

"Plus five for the *Clueless* reference. Now you're at negative fifteen," I send.

"I'm moving up in the world. So, not Laura, huh? Well, that's a blessing considering the last time I saw her she threatened to report me to HR for wearing Chucks to work."

"She's a work friend?"

"Ha! Friend. No. She's a former work associate who thought my job was completely superfluous."

There's clearly no love lost between them, and I internally rescind my sneeze curse on Laura Hepburn. She sounds unpleasant, but my ire for her has dissolved – miraculously – in the face of Eliot's distaste. What a cavewoman I apparently am.

"I thought you were a freelancer?" I message.

"So, you know a little bit about my work! Which means either we've worked together or we must have at least had surface small talk in the past."

"One of those things is true."

"Does that earn me five points?"

"Sure. You're obsessed with the points."

"I told you I'm competitive."

"You're the only one playing."

"That means it would be even more pathetic if I lose. I'm at negative ten now. What are other ways for me to get points?"

"Besides guessing who I am?"

"Yeah. How about if I make an accurate leap in logic then I get points. And . . . if I make you laugh I get points. Just for funsies."

Remember what I said about how he's just a big, handsome puppy? Well, this is officially the only time in my life I've ever had a crush on someone who said stuff like *funsies*. But somehow it works on him.

I'm currently sitting on my kitchen counter in a ball, balanced perfectly, about to roll off in a heap if he texts me one more cute thing. I'm going to have to stick to one-word answers here if I don't want him to know that his playfulness actually has me grinning like the Joker at my cell phone.

"Okay," I message.

And then, because I'm terrified of him getting bored, I add a quick:

"Good luck."

"So ominous. It's like you know for a fact that I'll never be able to successfully make you laugh."

Little does he know that for the past fifteen minutes I've been giggling like a maniac every time my cell phone buzzes. It would probably be cooler if I remained aloof. But like I said before, I'm nothing if not honest. So . . .

"I never cheat when I play games. So, in that case, I'm going to have to award some retroactive points and bring your total up to zero."

"To what do I owe the honor of these unexpected points? Wait! That means I already made you laugh at some point. Right?"

"Maybe."

"It was Clueless, right? Or no. Funsies. I definitely got you with funsies."

"Minus two points for arrogance."

"Crap! Good call. Good call. You're tough but fair."

"Gotta stay humble, Hoffman."

I instantly regret last-naming him. Is there anything that says you have a crush on a guy more than spontaneously last-naming him? If we were in high school, I'd be drawing a picture on the ground with my toe and twisting my hair around one finger. I'd be asking to wear his letterman's jacket. He's going to realize that he's accidentally texted his secret admirer and block my ass before his bunny gets boiled.

But he doesn't block me. Instead, he texts me back.

"*Good advice, JD.*"

"JD? Is that someone you know? Is it an official guess?"

"*No! You just used my last name so I wanted to use yours, but obviously I don't know yours so I used the last two letters of the way you're saved in my phone. Officially, your name according to me is Vplkjdjd. Or JD for short.*"

This little development has me hopping down off the counter and pacing from one side of the kitchen to the other. I've gotta move. I step into the living room and immediately backtrack into the kitchen. The sight of my blankets folded up on the couch makes me grimace.

My phone buzzes again in my hand. He's texted me again.

"*Hey, I'm not keeping you up too late, am I? I don't want to be a bother.*"

"No. I'm a night owl. If I weren't talking to you I'd probably be—"

Unfortunately my finger slips and I send the voice message before I finish it. And honestly, maybe it's a good thing my finger slipped because I was about to get real chatty.

"*You'd probably be what? You can't just cut off mid-sentence!*"

There's no way I'm telling him.

"Take a guess, then. It's an opportunity for points."

"*Ah. Okay, okay. I see where you're going with this. Okay, let me think. If you weren't talking to me you'd probably be . . . watching cringey dating shows on Netflix?*"

I jolt when I hear his message and stupidly glance around me as if he could magically be standing in my kitchen with me, observing my every move without me having previously noticed. I cannot believe he guessed it in one. It would be great if I was more into lying because I'd love to save face right now but . . .

"That's . . . some serious psychic shit right there," I message.

"*HAHAHAHAHAAAAAAAAAAAA!!*"

His entire message just consists of his hysterical laughter. I'm laughing, too. It's impossible not to. He texts again a moment later.

"*You're kidding. I was right? That's amazing. Gotta be worth at least fifty points, don't you think?*"

I make a valiant effort to swallow down my laughter.

"I'll give you twenty-five points. Twenty for the guess, and five for the laugh."

"*I am smoking this game. I'm gonna get to two hundred in an hour. Tops.*"

I sink down, my back sliding along the kitchen cabinets, and breathe deeply. There's no chance in hell I'll ever let him actually figure out who I am, but . . . he's down to do this for another hour?

"Seriously, though," I message. "How'd you guess that about the dating shows?"

"*Isn't that what everyone does when they can't sleep?*"

"Is that what you do when you can't sleep, Hoffman? Watch reality television?"

"*Lately. Are you watching the dating show where they're handcuffed together or the one where they're in masks?*"

"Handcuffs. The masks one is trash."

"*Really? Why? I liked the masks one!*"

"Because after their faces were revealed they all ended up being hot anyway. It's like, if you're gonna make people fall in love without seeing each other, why not cast normal-looking people, you know?"

"*Good point. Yeah. Now that I think about it, the show would have been way better if they'd been regular people. I guess nobody wants to see regular people fall in love.*"

"I do! And, I wouldn't exactly call what they did on that show 'love'."

"*Another good point. You've got a remarkably discriminating eye for reality television, JD.*"

"Thanks?"

"*Okay, considering you watched* Blinded Dates *in its entirety I'm going to take an educated guess based on viewership demographics and say that you're between the ages of twenty-five and forty.*"

"Five points."

"*Boom! Okay, I can now eliminate the middle-aged to elderly contingent of women in my life.*"

"You've got a lot of middle-aged to elderly women saved in your phone?"

"*I've got my mom and aunts. Most of my mom's friends. An old boss or two. A couple neighbors from my building. All in all, yeah. I'd say I have a very respectable number of older ladies saved in my phone.*"

"You sound proud of that."

"*I mean, I'm not NOT proud of it . . . Hey, JD?*"

"Yeah?"

"*You said you're a night owl. Is that a code word for insomniac?*"

"Maybe. Probably. I've never slept very much. Even as a kid."

"*So, you spend a lot of the night awake?*"

"Most nights. Yeah."

"*What's your trick for getting through it?*"

"What do you mean?"

"Well, usually I'm a champion sleeper. Like, asleep in under thirty seconds and don't move until my alarm goes off nine hours later. But lately . . . I guess I'm just wondering if you have any tricks for passing the time at night."

"Sure." I think for a second and then message again. "Let's see . . . there's the usual—reading, meditating, listening to podcasts. Those are if you're trying to coax yourself into sleep. But if you're at the point where you've completely given up on sleep . . . well, there's pedicures, dying your hair another color, trashy television, working out, chatting with some random dude over voice message . . ."

"Random dude, you say? I'd be offended if you hadn't just given me another hint. This conclusively means that you're not Marta, my tailor, or Sarah from the wine shop because I'm omnipresent enough in their lives for them to never just refer to me as a 'random dude'."

I'm torn between laughing and face-palming. Of course he's on familiar terms with a tailor and wine-shop lady. These are two types of establishment I've literally never set foot in once in my life. I've got the light beer in the fridge and the tattered hemlines to prove it. For the first time in this conversation, I really, truly, try to picture him in this exact second. I've been in his apartment a few times and the details come back to me with alarming clarity. I hadn't realized I'd been paying such close attention. But I can say with certainty that he's either lounging on that fancy gray couch in his living room or on his bed that's so high most people would need a step stool and carabiners just to hoist themselves onto it. His life is basically sponsored by Pottery Barn.

He wears three-piece suits for meetings with clients.

He drinks wine electively.

Once again my crush on this guy utterly baffles me. He couldn't be further from my usual type.

And I'm sure I'm a million miles away from his, but, as it's the witching hour and the only thing he needs to know about me is what my voice sounds like, does that really matter?

"How do you know you're the random dude I was referring to?"

"*Ha. Are you having more than one late-night voice message conversation right now?*"

"Maybe. I could be."

"*You're two-timing me already? Dang. And here I thought we had the juice to go the distance.*"

He's obviously joking as much as I am, but even so, his words have me pressing a smile into my kneecaps as I sit scrunched on the kitchen floor. For the first time in months, I'm actually glad that Pops isn't around. If he were, he'd be razzing me into next Tuesday over this cheesy grin of mine. This is the kind of smile that gets its way. I try to forcibly pull the corners of my mouth down but as soon as I let go, they're boinging back into a crescent moon.

"What can I say, Hoffman? I'm in high demand."

"*Well, I'll just have to find a way to distinguish myself from these other losers. How many points do they have?*"

"You realize you just referred to them as 'other losers'. Meaning that you yourself are also a loser, yes?"

"*I'm nothing if not honest with myself.*"

"Hoffman, you're not a loser."

"*JD, I was messaging my little sister in the middle of the night because I couldn't sleep. That makes me at least twenty percent loser.*"

Sister, he said? My brain immediately takes that little piece of information and strips it for parts. Was he just chatting? Or was he intentionally letting it slip that it was his sister he'd meant to message and not another woman? Does he want me to know that he wasn't booty-calling someone?

"No way. You're wrong."

"*You don't think that makes me a loser?*"

"No, I just think twenty percent was a little too high. I think it makes you fifteen percent loser."

"*You're a kind and benevolent god.*"

"I do my best."

I'm staring at my phone, waiting for another message to pop through and give me a happy little coronary when a distant—and unfortunately familiar—sound catches my ear.

It's next door's smoke alarm.

Oh, my God. This is literally the fourth time in two months that Mr. Sawyer has set off his alarm in the middle of the night. Apparently the man takes sleeping pills that knock him out but also give him a hankering for nighttime toast. I've lost count of the number of times I've reminded him to unplug his toaster before bed. It'll be T-minus thirty seconds before tiny, balding Mr. Sawyer is knocking on my door in slippers and a bathrobe, rubbing his eyes and telling me he has no idea what happened but there's smoke in his kitchen.

I consider going into the back bathroom and locking the door, letting Mr. Sawyer figure out his smoke alarm on his own for once. But then I think of Pops, hopefully getting a good night's rest in his care facility, trusting me to take care of the people around him. Pops wouldn't hide from Mr. Sawyer. Pops would already be pulling his boots on.

With a pained, disappointed sigh, I drag myself up off the kitchen floor.

"Hey, Eliot," I message him. "Unfortunately I have to go help somebody with something right now. It was nice talking to you, though. I hope you can get to sleep soon."

"*Oh! Sure. Yeah, it was nice talking to you, too. Good luck with . . . whatever you're doing.*"

Mr. Sawyer starts knocking on my door right on cue, and I

look mournfully at my phone one more time. I can't help myself from saying one last thing.

"Good night."

He messages back immediately.

"*Good night.*"

All right. Back to real life. I slip my phone in my pocket and answer the door.

Chapter Two

Eliot

I wasn't alone last night.

That's the first thought I have when I stir awake. There was someone there with me. A fellow insomniac. Another middle-of-the-night zombie staring at the ceiling. She talked to me. She probably didn't even realize she was doing it, but she actually talked me *through* it. Brought me through the worst part of the night. Ferried me across the river. Painlessly.

Have you ever had one of those random times of day when you always look at the clock? You know, you just happen to look up at 2:16 in the afternoon a couple times a week? You don't know why exactly, but you just do? Well, unfortunately, for the last two months, mine has been 4:27.

In the morning.

For years, I've always been a very disciplined sleeper. No screens after 9 p.m. Stretching, toothbrushing and flossing, lights out by eleven and generally I knock out for a solid eight or nine hours. Almost every night of my adult life.

But for the last two months? I'm a sweaty, red-eyed mess in and out of light sleep until the dreaded moment I look at the clock, and yup, it's 4:27 again.

4:27 is a real asshole, because it's too early to be considered morning and too late to be considered nighttime. If it was five o'clock on the dot, I'd just say it was time to get up for the day. If it was four o'clock on the dot, I'd try to convince myself to sleep a little more. But since it's a no-man's-land time of night, I usually just end up staring at my bedroom ceiling, listening for footsteps that don't come.

They *can't* come, I constantly have to remind myself. Security system, new locks on the windows, CCTV. I'm snug as a bug in my apartment.

But that doesn't mean I'm not jumping half an inch off the sheets every time my apartment building creaks. And though there have been a lot of renovations in the last five years, this building is *old*. It likes for its opinions to be heard. Every time there's even the slightest hint of humidity in the air, the building groans and complains and I'm left tossing and turning.

Last night, though? Last night was different. I got a couple hours of sleep after my unexpected texting conversation with Mystery Woman, AKA JD. Now, it's 5:15 and for the first time in forever, I snoozed right past 4:27. I sit up, scratch the back of my head, and eye my phone on the nightstand. There's no way she messaged me while I was asleep, right?

I nudge my phone, wake it up, but nothing but the block-numbered time looks back at me. No messages.

It would have been crazy to assume that there'd be a message from her. Why would she voluntarily reach out to the random guy who'd been pestering her at odd hours of the night? Frankly, it's a miracle she talked to me as long as she did.

My thumb is momentarily possessed by a ghost and hits the replay button on her last message to me. Her voice echoes out of my phone.

"*Good night.*"

That's a nice voice right there. There's a low, husky quality to it, like she's halfway between a dream and reality. And so familiar. Where have I heard that voice before? I know this woman. I just don't know *how* I know this woman.

Why, you ask? *How*, you ask? How is it possible that I could feel that I almost certainly know this person but I just can't place her?

Well, I have a very . . . unique brain. One that I've come to love in my adult years. Now that I know how to manage my life, the way my brain works is actually a real positive. But there are definitely things I've learned to avoid for my own sanity. And the question of who this JD person really is is the kind of thing that will plop itself down in the middle of my frontal lobe and start paying rent.

I'm the type of person who has to have child locks on my internet so that I can only access work-related sites during the workday. I didn't trust myself to upgrade from a flip phone for years because I knew that if I had a movie theater, video game console, a camera, and an internet connection in my pocket at all times, I would immediately sink my career.

I get fixated on things. And it's never the right things. I know that if I want to get any work done at all today I have to mentally put JD in a box and throw away the key.

No. That's too sinister.

Sitting on the edge of my bed I practice one of the many visualization exercises my therapist has helped me with. I close my eyes and picture JD. Which is ridiculous, because I have no idea what she looks like. She's an animated silhouette of a woman. Not tall, not short, not curvy, not skinny. She's a she-blob. Then, in my mind, I offer an elbow and lead her to a car. She was funny and cute so I make sure the car is cool. How about an old-school Camaro? Candy apple red. I open the driver's seat door and help her in. *Drive safe*, I tell her in my mind, *see you after work*. I wave while the silhouette drives the Camaro out of sight.

There. That oughtta do it. I'll think about JD when I'm done with my workday.

Ten hours later, the very second I close my computer for the day, the Camaro is squealing back into the parking lot of my frontal lobe. I mostly work from home so at five o'clock on the dot I'm already standing in my kitchen, staring blankly into a fridge full of produce while my brain is neck-deep in the mystery of who this woman is.

She's someone I know well enough to recognize her voice, but not well enough to have called or texted her before last night.

Unfortunately, the whole random letters instead of an actual contact name is a fairly common occurrence for me. One of the things that's special about my brain is that letters and numbers are really hard for me to decipher. Dyslexia is what they called it when I was growing up. But once I made it to college and had access to student services I was diagnosed with a whole slew of other learning disorders as well. The long and short is that concentrating doesn't come naturally to me and neither does reading.

Having someone watch me while I hunt and peck my approximated guess at how to spell their name into my contacts list is basically my worst nightmare. Generally when I have a new person to add to my address book I just jab at a random mix of letters to save face and then the second I'm alone, I go back and fix it at my leisure, un-surveilled. Unfortunately, I have occasionally forgotten to go back and fix it in the past. And JD is one of those casualties. At some point, I stood next to her, heard her name, and pretended to input it into my phone.

I paw through my fridge and frown when I see that I have everything I need for chicken stir-fry except for the chicken. How did that happen? I'm usually so meticulous with my grocery list. Ah. My sister, Vera, came over earlier this week, and instead of making chicken quesadillas for one, I made them for two.

I grab my house keys and make the jog down to the grocery store around the corner.

"Hey, Eliot."

I smile at Dawn, my usual checkout person, and look back at my phone, checking for messages from JD. Then I do a double-take. Dawn is about twenty-five, pretty cute, always swimming in her store-issued employee vest. Have I ever taken her number? I can't remember. I replay her voice in my head. Is that JD's voice? I only realize I'm staring when Dawn starts blushing. She's glancing up at me from under her bangs and fumbling to get the package of chicken breasts to scan. I have to hear her voice again to be sure.

"How's your day been?" I ask her.

"Good!" she squeaks, blushing even more.

This doesn't sound like JD's voice from last night. But I can't quite tell. Why is she squeaking? Is it because she's embarrassed to have spent last night unexpectedly talking to me for an hour, or is it because . . .

Oh. I catch sight of my face on the CCTV screen behind the cashier's stand and realize immediately that Dawn is probably blushing because I'm staring at her like I'm about to dissect her with a microscope and tweezers. I look like a lunatic.

"Have a good night!" I wave gently and try to look non-threatening as I leave the grocery store.

I mentally cross Dawn off the list on the jog back to my apartment.

I'm back, standing in my kitchen, frowning at the just-bought packet of chicken, when I realize that I don't want chicken stir-fry for dinner. I want Thai food. Frustrated with myself, I tug at my hair a little, debating what to do. Usually, I completely shut down these kinds of impulsive urges. Impulsivity is something I've grappled with my whole life and up until I finally paid it off three years ago, I had the credit card debt to prove it. I live life according to a very strict plan, all the way down to my menu for the week, or else I end up spending five hundred dollars on takeout in a single month.

I put the chicken in the fridge and check my bank balance. Next, I look at the whiteboard on the wall that has my menu for the week planned out. Lastly, I check my debit transactions to see when the last time I ordered takeout was.

I decide that it wouldn't be completely irresponsible to order in tonight. I can have the stir-fry tomorrow night. I call in my usual order at the Thai place down the block and spend the next twenty minutes passing my phone from one hand to the other, pondering who JD might really be.

That woman I met at Chelsea market before Christmas-time? I got her number, didn't I? She was a self-published author who had been interested in my design services for her next book. What was her name again? Jackie? Jessica? But I'm pretty sure she'd been wearing a wedding band so that probably means she wouldn't have stayed up into the wee hours of the night halfway flirting with me, right?

I check my phone and don't find a Jackie or a Jessica. So, I guess it could be her.

My doorbell rings and I grab cash from my wallet. When I swing open the door I'm surprised to see that instead of the usual delivery kid, it's actually the Thai restaurant's hostess who is standing there. She has long, pretty hair and a nervous smile.

"Hi, your brother's not delivering tonight?"

"He's out on a delivery and your order was up, so I thought I'd just run it around the corner for you."

"Thanks." I hand over the cash and a nice tip and take the food. "That's really thoughtful of you."

"Mmhmm." She's looking down and playing with the zipper on her raincoat.

It's time for her to go now, but she's still just standing there. I hesitate with my hand on the door. Finally she sighs and rocks back on her heels, her eyes still bottoming out somewhere around my throat. "Have a good night."

And then she's hurrying back toward the elevator and disappearing behind the sliding doors.

I look at the Thai food in my hand and back at the elevator. At the Thai food and at the elevator.

Hmmm.

I think about messaging JD and asking if she just delivered me my dinner, but 1) I'm not sure if this messaging thing was a one-night-only type of deal, and 2) I'm scared of how many points she might deduct if that's a wrong guess.

I eat my dinner slowly, quietly, at the dinner table, refusing to let myself multitask. One of the best ways I've found to manage my chaotic brain is to only let myself do one thing at a time, focusing as best I can on that single task. But my phone is calling my name from the kitchen counter.

After dinner I go for a run, do ten minutes of stretching, shower, pick up clutter in my living room, vacuum, and answer four different work emails.

I deserve an Oscar for my emulation of a functioning adult this evening. Because even though I've gone through the motions, if pondering JD's identity were a video game, I'd be permanently acquainting my couch with the imprint of my ass.

My fingers would be irrevocably curved into gamer claws right now, empty Red Bull cans scattered across the floor.

But luckily for my poor fingers, she's not a video game. Instead, I'm staring out the window at 9:15 in the evening, refusing on principle to grab my phone to message a strange woman I don't know, and avoiding the irrefutable fact that there is absolutely nothing to do but go to bed—and absolutely zero chance that I'll fall asleep when I do.

Another night of dating shows in bed it is.

I'm on hour four of a show about people who are trying to find love—get this—*Little Mermaid*-style. AKA they can't speak to one another. My eyelids are, miracle of miracles, starting to get a little heavy, so I'm just contemplating shutting my laptop when my phone buzzes on the nightstand.

I scramble for it, catching it up before it even stops vibrating, and there, look at that, holy smokes, *yes*, oh my GOD, it's a voice message text from JD.

Chapter Three

Eliot

"Awake tonight, too?"

She. Just. Messaged. Me.

Somehow, in the last ten seconds I've gone from collapsed into a pile of pillows to standing straight up on my bed. If I lifted my hand over my head, I could plant a palm on the ceiling. I'm completely crackers. I fall into a crouch and then tip awkwardly onto one side when my squishy mattress betrays me.

"Every night."

I sound breathless in my message to her, but that's because I *am* breathless. I was fairly certain I wasn't going to hear from her again. But she messaged me. She messaged ME. I'm now a million miles from sleep. I can feel my heart beating in my ears. I couldn't care less.

"Wasn't sure I'd catch you, but I thought I'd give it a shot."

"I'm glad you did!"

I sound way too excited, but them's the breaks. I *am* too excited. Even though I have no idea who this woman is, she's my comrade in the trenches of insomnia. For months, it's just been me and my Netflix account. But right now? I have a living, breathing person, who not only is talking to me, she understands the peculiar estrangement of not being able to sleep at night. She's as fried as I am.

My glee starts to subside when five minutes pass and there's no response from her. Was I too gung ho? I've been known to want things a little too badly. It's part of my chemistry. It goes with the whole obsessing over random stuff thing.

"You still there?" I ask her.

"*Yes! Sorry. Someone just needed my attention for a second. But it's all good now.*"

I frown.

"Same person as last night?"

"*No.*"

I frown more. I thought for sure she was joking last night when she said that she'd been voice-messaging with someone else as well, because, duh, is there anyone else in the world besides me who prefers voice-messaging over texting? But . . . maybe . . . is she *actually* talking with someone else at the same time she's talking to me?

Well, if she is, I guess that's exactly zero of my business.

"I'm glad you messaged me tonight. I was getting dangerously close to finishing season 1 of Love on Mute all in one fell swoop."

"*Yikes, things are getting dark over there, Hoffman.*"

"You're telling me. This show is terrible. The worst one yet."

"*Maybe we need to switch it up from dating shows. I mean, there's more out there, right?*"

I'm grinning at my phone, up on my side, balancing my cheek on one palm. I'm very aware of the fact that in between messaging her, I keep placing my phone in the center of the other pillow. It's a place of honor. It's where someone else's head is supposed to go.

"Switch it up?" I ask. "It's not like we're searching for high art, are we? And what's more mindless than competitive dating shows?"

"*Hmm. Competitive baking shows?*"

"Actually, I've been meaning to watch the British one that everyone is always talking about."

"*Yeah, me too. People say it's soothing.*"

"Well, shall we?"

I can hear the heartbeat in the palm of my hand as I prop my head up. All I did was ask her to watch a television show with me, but even so, I suddenly have a case of sweaty pits.

"*Shall we what?*"

"Watch that baking show together?"

"*Define 'together'.*"

I laugh at how flat and unimpressed her voice sounds. For some reason, it delights me.

"I don't know, we press play at the same time and chat while we watch?"

There's a long pause, and I brace myself for her to message me back and tell me that I'm being too . . . much.

"*Which episode should we start with? Looks like there's a lot of seasons and, like, preseasons and Christmas specials and stuff.*"

I scramble for my computer so fast I knock it off the bed. It's times like these that I feel like a third-grader in a man's body. There are moments in my life when I could swear I haven't grown up at all. And feet balancing on the bed, one hand planted on the floor, reaching with my fingertips for something I just dropped while my blankets tangle around my legs is definitely one of those times.

As I gather it back up, I take a deep breath. I peruse the options for the baking show, and we decide on an episode, coordinating to press play at the same moment. Plucky music and colorful baked goods fill my screen. I get a message from JD and pause the show to listen to it.

"*Crap. This is backfiring. Instead of making me sleepy, it's making me hungry.*"

"I know. I haven't eaten a cupcake in about a decade, but suddenly I feel like I'd faceplant into one given the chance."

"*You haven't eaten a cupcake in a decade? Are you shitting me?*"

"Just health-conscious. Sugar and dyes make me lose it."

"*Like what kind of losing it?*"

"Like seeing spots in my vision and tapping my fingers a mile a minute and impulse-buying egg boilers off the home shopping network."

"*That . . . is a very specific type of losing it. Oh, shit! That was such a sick burn from that old lady judge.*"

"What? What burn? They haven't even started judging yet."

"*Huh? Wait, what minute are you on?*"

I realize the issue immediately and am already exiting out of our text strand and calling her number before I can think twice.

Chapter Four

"Um. Hello? Hoffman?"

"Hi."

"Why . . . are you calling?"

"Yeah. Um. Sorry. Sort of impulsive on my part, but I realized that we were messaging at different rates and messing up the show."

"Huh?"

"I was pausing the show each time I sent or received a message, and I'm guessing you weren't?"

"Nope."

"So, I'm a few minutes behind you."

"Oh, okay, what minute are you on? I'll rewind."

". . ."

"Eliot?"

"Sorry! Yeah, I'm on minute twelve and forty-two seconds. I . . . really didn't expect you to play along with me on this one."

"It's two in the morning and I'm clearly not about to fall asleep, what else is there to do?"

"Hey, JD?"

"Yeah?"

"We've definitely met in person before, right?"

"That information will cost you, hmmm, ten points at least."

"Deal."

"Yes, we've definitely met in person."

"Best ten points I've ever spent. Hey, JD?"

"Yes, Eliot."

"Ha. You know, I may not know who you are, but I can definitely tell when you're rolling your eyes. Anyway. Thanks for watching with me. Sometimes I feel like I'm the only person in the world left awake on nights like this."

"I'm awake, too. I can pretty much guarantee it. I'm always awake."

"Good thing we have people making bread to soothe us into sleep."

"Good thing."

Chapter Five

Jessie

Welp. I just woke up with my cell phone plastered to my cheek and my out of battery laptop halfway balanced on my stomach. Because apparently I fell asleep on the phone last night.

Talking to Eliot Hoffman. While we watched a show together.

It's so nauseatingly high school. Which must be the reason I immediately bury my face in the couch cushions and make a noise I haven't made for fifteen years.

What am I doing? I'm off the deep end.

Okay.

It's probably time I explain something.

I'm very likely not Eliot Hoffman's type. I am a very specific . . . flavor, shall we say? And when dudes aren't into me, they are like, *viscerally* not into me. I don't say that from a place of insecurity. Honestly, it reassures me. Because when someone is expressing interest, I know that they are really into it. Me. And if they aren't then there's no confusion and we all move on. It's a black-and-white system and it works for me.

In the handful of times that I've stood in front of or next to Eliot Hoffman, and in the fewer than a handful of times I've actually spoken with him, I've never once gotten a vibe that he was into me. He obviously likes talking to me on the phone. But if he were to see me in person, he'd probably weed-whack the flirty vibe immediately.

But this . . . this is not why I'm refusing to tell him who I am. If it were as simple as that, I'd pull off the Band-Aid and let the chips fall where they may.

The anonymity is necessary, because when he finds out who I am . . . at some point, he's going to find out who my brother is. And that's when things get ugly.

Like, *very* ugly.

As in, my entire life completely unravels. I go broke and homeless. My brother disappears off the face of the earth. And Eliot Hoffman hates me and never speaks to me again.

Did I mention that the stakes are kind of high?

So, why, oh why am I doing something as stupid as falling asleep on the phone with him? Why, oh why am I not just screening his calls? Or blocking him and pretending that this whole mess never even happened?

Because I'm possessed by this stupid, crushed-out girl, and she takes control of my body so she can flirt with him.

Frustrated, I peel myself off the couch and hop directly into some workout clothes. I take a deep breath as I step outside my building and stretch one quad and then the other. It's early yet, and as it's mid-April, there's night-frost on the few tulips that have bloomed in the tree wells. There are a few early-morning commuters headed up Bedford toward the trains, but for the most part, I have the sidewalk to myself as I set off at a jog.

The air still has that sleepy, dawn-ish feeling about it where everything feels like a secret. My footsteps are loud as I run past all the houses where people are still tucked into their beds. Here's the thing. I don't sleep well, and of course, I wish I could sleep better. But part of me also likes being awake when everyone else is asleep. It makes me feel like I know something that almost no one else does. If the aliens came right now, at this very second, I'd be the one they'd see first. The top of my head bopping along as I jog down the street. Everyone's asleep and I'm on neighborhood watch. Look at me, holding down the fort for all these sleeping strangers. It's a good feeling.

I get to the gym just as Raoul is opening up the security gate.

"Hey, kid." His tawny skin crinkles into smile lines but his mouth stays serious. He's not surprised to see me.

I've only known him for the few months since I moved to this neighborhood to take over for Pops, but Raoul is one of those people who shows you everything at once. Once you know him, you know him. He didn't bat an eye when I showed up that first day, even though I was surely one of the very few women to ever ask for a membership at his gym.

Geddy's is not a designer gym. This isn't where you go on January third to maximize your weight-loss potential. They don't sell expensive water at the front desk or put fancy shampoo in the showers. Your membership buys you access to the equipment, exactly one scratchy towel a visit, and if you're lucky, some one-on-one time with Raoul Geddy himself.

Geddy's is where you go if you want someone to step on your back when you're doing pushups. It's where you go if you want to beat the shit out of a punching bag. It's where you go if when you split the skin on your knuckles, you want an old man to superglue the cut closed.

Pops is the one who first taught me how to box. And until I moved down here earlier this winter, I was still going to our same boxing gym up in Queens. I'd still prefer Pops as my boxing coach, but Raoul is a steady second. He's tough and nonjudgmental and never lets up about my form'.

I help him flick on the lights, and we stretch in silence for a little bit before he grabs the jump ropes for us. During the days, he's there as a coach, helping the members through their workouts. But in the mornings, he works out, too. Which is why I started coming in the morning. It's nice to push myself alongside him. Two minutes pass, and he's already embarrassing me. He's a sixty-eight-year-old man jumping rope so fast it's just a blur, and I'm the one sucking wind. He grabs the pads and gloves and has me start out with a few combinations. The *thwack* of my gloves against the pads is the only sound for a long time.

"How's the old man?"

Pops started coming to this gym after he moved down from Queens ten years ago, so they know one another really well.

"His spirits are high. You know him. But the chemo's just wrecking him."

Raoul grunts. "You getting up there to visit him?"

"Not as much as I'd like. A couple times a week. I'd like to go every day."

"But you've got a lot of work to get done at the house, huh?"

"Yeah. Seems like every time I turn around there's something else to do."

"You ever need help, I'll send my boy over."

I make a noncommittal sound. I don't want to be ungrateful to Raoul, and it's nice of him to offer. But recently I've started to get the feeling that he wants to set me up with his son. And Ronnie? Ronnie is cool. Big and shy. Every once in a while I'll catch him sneaking peeks at me from the other side of the gym. He's exactly who I should have a crush on.

But even though my physical body is sweatily running through combinations in a stinky gym, my inner crush is somewhere in a bubble bath, chewing toxically pink bubble gum and watching reruns of *Sex and the City*. On the outside, I'm a tough cookie. On the inside I'm pure candy.

This is my only explanation for my feelings for Eliot Hoffman.

Who I talked to for hours last night.

Just for funsies.

"Yow." Raoul steps back and shakes out one of his hands. "You put some power behind that one."

"Sorry."

"Don't be."

I use my teeth to start taking the tape off my gloves. I can feel Raoul watching me.

"Everything all right?" he asks.

I grunt.

"Is it Jack?" he asks.

I look up at him in surprise.

"Don't look so surprised. Whenever your dad was in here hitting me too hard it was always because of your brother. It figures that he might be an issue for you, too."

I sigh, consider evading. But I hate keeping secrets. And these days that really feels like all I do. I'm keeping secrets for Pops around the house. I'm keeping secrets from Eliot about who I am. Adding Raoul to the list just seems like unnecessary torture.

"Jack may or may not have created a situation that I am now paying the price for."

"What kind of price?"

Raoul is five-foot-five on a good day, maybe a buck-twenty after Thanksgiving dinner. But right now there's a metallic glint in his eyes and I could swear he just grew by an inch or two.

"No, no. Nothing like that. He didn't get me in trouble with the law. Or with anybody scary or anything. I'm just out here lying to cover his ass." I occupy myself with the last bits of tape on my gloves. "To somebody I really don't want to be lying to."

Raoul opens his mouth to say something, but before he can, the door to the gym swings open and three strapping young gents pile inside.

"I gotta get going," I tell Raoul. "Got stuff to do."

"Go easy on yourself," he tells me and I can see from the look in his eye that he really means it. That's the medicine he's prescribing. *You're not a punching bag. Come to the gym if you need to beat something up.*

I give him a nod, quickly wipe down my gear, and lock it back into my locker.

I'm halfway home when I see Eliot Hoffman up the block. I knew this might happen, considering how close we live to one another. My heart lurches sideways, and even though he's walking away from me, I still cross the street to get further away from him. He's got a to-go coffee in one hand, and I can tell from the fancy paper cup that he went to that one café that has the five-dollar almond croissants and the Instagram-ready baristas. I bet they flirt with him relentlessly as they hand over his latte. I bet they put on lipstick just so they can leave a kiss on the side of his cup. He probably scores a new number every morning.

He stops at the intersection and glances behind him. I'm so glad I crossed the street because he would have seen me otherwise. Well, he'd have seen the me that isn't me. I mean, he'd have seen the me he knows me as, not the me he doesn't know I am.

Are you confused yet?

I am.

Either way, I'm glad he isn't currently looking at the me

who's all sweaty from the gym while he stands there in slacks and a button-down and looking like he'd just naturally smell like the inside of a new car.

The light changes and he strolls away. I mentally slap myself and head home. If I get my work done fast enough today I'll have time to visit Pops. And that's all that matters right now.

Chapter Six

Eliot

Have you ever woken up the way they do in television shows? Where you sit straight up and your hair sticks out in every direction and you nearly fall out of bed, but that's okay because you've had the epiphany of a lifetime and suddenly everything in your life becomes crystal-clear?

Well, that happened to me this morning.

Last night JD fell asleep on the phone with me. I hung up, playing the sound of her voice in my head over and over until I drifted into sleep. And then, I woke up this morning like a bolt of lightning had just hit me.

I knew exactly who she was.

I had just enough time to get ready for work, get out and test my theory, and then get back in time for a conference call I had scheduled.

I don't want to be sweaty when I roll up to the coffee shop, which is the only reason I don't jog there. When I get there, I stand to one side of the windows so she can't see. I shake out my fingers like a major league pitcher. I'm so freaking nervous I could probably take a sip of lemonade and turn it back into a lemon in my mouth.

Well, now or never.

I take a deep breath and push into the café. It's a cute place, I guess. Newish in the neighborhood, everything is powder-blue and gold, and I'd probably come here more often if it wasn't so expensive. But I don't care about that right now. I'd pay fifty bucks for a single stale scone if it means I get to see JD.

Please let her be working today. Please let her be working today.

At first glance, my stomach drops because I don't see her. But then, yes! She stands up from behind the counter with a stack of to-go cups balanced in her hand. Her red hair is braided neatly down her back, and she looks as cute as ever in her powder-blue apron.

She doesn't see me at first but when she catches sight of me standing two customers back in the line, her face lights up. I clear my throat when I make it to the front.

"Hey, Mia."

"You remembered my name!" There's that familiar voice. Husky. Honey. I'm almost positive she's JD. But then she speaks again. "And you're . . . hold on, give me a second." She cocks her head to one side. "Ethan?"

My stomach drops again. Either she's not JD or she's a sensational actor. Because she genuinely looks like she doesn't remember my name.

"Eliot."

"Right! Hey, did you ever make it to that concert? The one we talked about before?"

The one other time we ever spoke in person was about two months ago. She was on her way out of work and was wearing a T-shirt for a band, and we got to talking about their music. She mentioned they had a concert coming up, and I hadn't been sure if she was suggesting we go together or not.

"Uh, nope. No."

"Me either." Her smile widens. "You look nice today."

"Thanks."

I might have spent a few minutes extra getting my hair right. I also might have broken out a new shirt I haven't had a reason to wear yet.

But that was because I was pretty sure I was coming to see JD. But Mia . . . I gave her my phone number, right? I'm almost positive. But now that I'm here, looking right at her, I can't remember whether or not she gave me hers.

In which case, she might not be in my phone, jumbled contact info or not.

I order my drink and step off to the side. I look out the window at the passing neighborhood, but I'm pretty sure I can feel her eyes on the back of my head. When she calls my name, I smile as I take my drink from her. And there, in pen on the side of the blue paper cup, is a phone number.

I'll compare the numbers when I get home and can do it without an audience, but I already know that she's not JD. Why would JD give me her number? She would clearly already know that I had it.

Unless this is all just an elaborate ruse to throw me off her trail?

I take one last look at her as I walk out of the coffee shop. She smiles at me and it's flirtatious but not . . . knowing.

Odds are low that I've found JD.

I walk past the Thai restaurant on my way home but it won't open until lunchtime. I know that the family who owns it lives in the apartment above it. Is the hostess who delivered my dinner JD?

Ten minutes later I'm sitting in my home office and looking at the black screen of my laptop. The second I turn it on, I will only allow myself to think about work. I'll have to put JD in that Camaro again.

I open my phone and scroll through my contacts, hoping that seeing the blur of names zing past will somehow trigger some lost memory or clue as to how I know JD. I stop the scroll of contacts at random and find I'm staring at Paloma's contact info. My sister's best friend.

I groan. I hadn't even started to consider all of Vera's friends. I scroll again and land on an old friend of mine from college. Another groan. There are literally dozens of people that JD could be.

She could be an old work contact. She could be a buddy's ex-girlfriend. She could be someone I met on that cruise three years ago. Or worse, she could be someone totally random. What if I met her at a bar or a party and she's completely lost to the annals of time? When she tells me her name, I *still* might not know who she is. What if I'm trying to guess someone I truly don't know? I'll never find out who she is.

I take a deep breath and wave goodbye to JD for the day, flicking on my computer and setting my phone aside.

Around lunchtime I'm roused from work by someone knocking on my front door. I swing it open and blink at my superintendent standing on the other side.

If we're being honest here, my super kind of scares the shit out of me. She suffers exactly zero fools. She wears red-black lipstick and has tattoos up and down her arms. She's always in overalls and combat boots and has one of those middle-of-the-nose piercings. I have literally seen her with a pack of cigarettes rolled up into the sleeve of her white T-shirt. She's more James Dean than I could ever hope to be in my whole Windsor-knotted life.

I always feel like a complete square whenever I'm around her. Especially since the way we met was . . . God. I cringe just thinking about it. Let's just say that I didn't get her name, and I've been too scared to ask again.

I resist the urge to fiddle with the sleeves of my button-down. "Hey! What's up?"

Frida Hawkins, my downstairs neighbor, peeks around the door, her milk-white hair standing out against her tan skin. I hadn't even seen her standing there.

"Eliot. Hi there, sweetie."

"Hi, Frida."

"Your kitchen sink is leaking again and ruining my ceiling."

"Oh! Shoot!" This happened last year, too.

My super raises her eyebrows and holds up the toolbox I hadn't noticed she was carrying.

"Right, right." I'm shuffling to the side and waving her inside. Of course, because she has never in her life missed an opportunity to snoop, Frida ducks into my apartment as well, the top of her head bobbing past at my shoulder level. As soon as she gets inside she's immediately twisting one of my plants ninety degrees and straightening the mail on my countertop.

"I'm sure it won't take long," Frida assures me. "Do you have anything for us to drink?"

I glance over at the super who's looking pretty amused at Frida. I immediately take notes on how to smile and look like a complete badass at the same time.

"Sure, sure. Orange juice okay for everybody?"

The super nods and crouches down in front of my sink, getting to work. I spend the next twenty minutes gently herding Frida back toward the kitchen. If left to her own devices, I have zero doubts she would have already pawed through my underwear drawer.

Apparently the work is done because the super stands up,

washes her hands, and then polishes off the full glass of orange juice I left for her in three gigantic swallows. I bet she's one of those people who can parallel park in one swoop.

"Oh!" I remember at the last minute. "Actually, the light in my hallway has been flickering in and out. Do you have a second to check it out?"

"Really?" Frida asks at my elbow and I jump. The woman is sneaky like a cat. "Do you think it's the wiring? Maybe that security system you had installed is screwing with the electric."

I try very hard not to frown at Frida, but I don't like the reminder that the installation of my high-tech security system has definitely been quite the meal for the building gossips. I already feel silly enough every time I get home and come eye-to-eye with the red blinking light that tells me the system is activated. Knowing my neighbors are talking about it makes me feel even more sheepish.

"I'm pretty sure the two systems don't have anything to do with each other." By the time I'm done saying this to Frida, the super's already pulled one of my kitchen stools into the hallway and is unscrewing the light fixture. She eyes the flickering bulb for a second and then reaches up and screws it all the way in. The light immediately beams out, steady and strong.

Oh, my God. I don't resist the urge to cover my face with one hand. That . . . is . . . embarrassing.

I've lived with a flickering hall light for a month and a half now and it didn't even occur to me that maybe I hadn't screwed the bulb in far enough.

"I . . . right. Sorry. I'll . . . um, check that next time. Thanks."

I'm pretty sure she's trying not to smile as she puts the stool back and gives me a polite nod.

"I guess we'll be going now, Eliot." Frida reaches up to pat my face none too gently. "You should come by for dinner this week. Bring your sister. But don't bring that Patricia person, please. She was too much for me last time. What a talker. I couldn't get a word in edgewise."

This time, I'm the one trying to hold back a smile. Patricia was a woman I dated for a few months a few years ago, and she was, in a fact, a talker. Which was the exact reason I brought her for dinner at Frida's. Call it morbid curiosity, but I'd wanted to see what would happen when two titans clashed. Who would win the race for more words uttered in one night, Frida or Patricia? Patricia won, by a hair, and Frida will never let me forget it. I think every time I've seen her since she's found a way to mention that she doesn't think Patricia is the right girl for me. Incidentally, she's right. Patricia was not the right girl for me.

But conceding that point to Frida feels like conceding a little too much power over my dating life. I really don't want Frida to start feeling like she has influence over who I do or don't date. I can only imagine the blind dates she'd try to set me up on.

"Uh-huh." I'm at the door, holding it open for them. "Thanks again for the help."

The super, schlepping her toolbox, gives me a salute and a friendly smirk on her way out the door and somehow manages to make it look cool. I attempt to salute back and end up looking like a complete tool.

Frida smothers a laugh and gives me one more face slap disguised as affection. "A thumbs-up is more your speed, dear."

It's the wickedest burn anyone has ever given me. I can't help but laugh.

Chapter Seven

"Hey! Hi! I wasn't sure you'd call tonight, JD."

"I called to say sorry."

"For what?"

"For falling asleep last night."

"You're sorry for that? Isn't that kind of the point of what we're doing here? Killing time before we fall asleep?"

"Oh. Yeah. I guess I hadn't thought about it that way."

"In my opinion, the baking show was a winner. Entertaining enough to give us something to talk about and relaxing enough to knock us out. I hope there're, like, a hundred seasons."

"I really hope it doesn't take you a hundred seasons to get your sleeping issues figured out. What's that noise?"

"I'm washing paintbrushes."

"What kind?"

". . . the kind you use for painting?"

"You don't say. No, I mean, what were you painting? Like, your walls? Or a canvas?"

"Oh! Right. I was doing some watercoloring."

"Good, because in my experience painting your walls in the middle of the night never ends up being a good idea."

"I take it you've made some questionable color choices in the past?"

"That's how I ended up with a blood-red bedroom a few years back."

"There's something very . . . King Henry the Eighth about a red bedroom."

"You mean the king who killed all his wives?"

"Yeah. I can't quite put my finger on it. But it's kinda like, is it possible to have a blood-red bedroom and not sleep in a velvet robe? I don't think so."

"You're deeply weird, Hoffman."

"You're the one with the red bedroom."

"It only lasted until the paint dried, and then I promptly painted over it. Anyway, I didn't know you did watercolors."

"Yup. Some oils, too."

"How'd you get into that?"

"Well, there were some fine arts courses required for my graphic design major. But even before that I was drawing and painting all the time. My parents had this thing on the weekends when we were little that Saturday and Sunday mornings were supposed to be for quiet activities. So, my parents and my sister would usually read, and I would draw. Once they realized that art would keep me quiet for more than five consecutive minutes, they always made sure I had all the supplies I'd need."

"The way you talk about your family, it seems like you guys are close."

"Yeah. My sister and I are. She only lives a few blocks away from me. And my parents are really good people. They can be a little . . . too involved, I guess you'd say? So, over the last few years I've had to put up some . . . I guess you could call them boundaries. Which means that maybe we're not as close as we used to be, but it's a good trade because I no longer have to suppress the urge to tear my hair out whenever we talk."

"What kind of boundaries?"

"Oh, well, my mother would still be coming over to do my laundry if I let her. At one point she was trying to convince me to pay extra for this grocery delivery service because that way she could make the grocery list online for me, and she'd never have to worry about whether or not I had enough milk. What else . . . oh! For a long time, I thought my dad was just really interested in the ins and outs of my job because he'd call almost every day to talk about this deadline or that project. And then I eventually realized that he was taking meticulous notes on everything I was telling him and he was really calling to make sure that I was getting all my work done on time."

"Wow. That's . . . wow."

"It's all done from a place of love. But they can just be a bit much. Why are you laughing?"

"Just . . . my dad is pretty nosy, too."

"He's super involved in your life?"

"Yeah. Not the same way your parents are. He loves to know what's going on in my life. Gossip-wise. And he took, like, crazy good care of us while we were growing up. But the second I was out of the house after graduation, it was like, kid, manage your own life. Kind of a life-lesson thing, I think. He really wanted us to be able to handle stuff on our own. If I ever come to him with a problem, he'll listen, but if I don't mention it, he definitely doesn't offer an opinion."

"That sounds freaking wonderful."

"He's pretty great."

"Do you have any siblings?"

"Yeah. I have a brother. Hey, uh, what was the painting you were working on?"

"Oh. Ah . . ."

"What's the pause for? Is it something embarrassing?"

"No. Not exactly."

"Lemme guess. Nude self-portrait?"

"That's your *first guess* for what I'd be painting? Oh, my God. I must have made a weird first impression on you when we met."

"So, that's a no on the nude self-portrait?"

"I can honestly tell you right now that I have never painted a nude self-portrait in my life. Nor do I plan to."

"Shame."

"It's a shame?"

"Sure. You're a looker, Hoffman. People would probably pay good money for a nudie."

"You're saying something that sounds like a compliment, but I'm one hundred percent sure that you're making fun of me right now."

"Five points for the astute observation."

"This point system is starting to make me feel like I'm a puppy and you're my owner. Maybe I shouldn't be so easily manipulated by imaginary currency."

"I'll give you twenty points right now if you tell me what you were painting."

". . ."

"Eliot?"

"I'm thinking!"

"Haahhaha. I thought you were gonna start rejecting the point system."

"Twenty is a lot of points! I don't want to pass up this opportunity just to take a stand."

"I'm feeling generous. I'll make it twenty-five."

"Done. Okay. I was painting some concept frames for this other project I'm involved in."

". . ."

"JD?"

"I'm not giving you twenty-five points for that non-answer."

"But I told you the truth!"

"I still have no idea what you're talking about. What's a concept frame? What's the other project? What's the subject of the painting?"

"Playing hardball, I see."

"Cough up the deets, Hoffman."

"Okay, okay. I kind of . . . do this webcomic thing."

"What do you mean, 'webcomic thing'?"

"I mean that I'm the author and creator of one."

"You create the story and do all the artwork and stuff?"

"Yeah. Well, most of it. I do a lot of the artwork on a design tablet, but first, when I'm still working everything out, I do concept frames on paper. When I get to the color-blocking parts, I often use watercolors to see what I like."

"That is . . . really cool."

"Really?"

"Seriously, it's way cooler than I thought you were. You've just upped your game by about a hundred degrees."

"Ha. I thought you'd think it was nerdy."

"Nerdy stuff becomes cool once you're out of high school. What's the name of the webcomic?"

"Why?"

"Because I obviously want to search it."

"Nah. That's okay. I have enough readers already."

"Spill! Why aren't you telling me?"

"Well, I guess, to be honest, because I've never told anyone else? I kinda do the whole thing anonymously."

"Oh. Okay, well, I don't want to force you to tell me then. I obviously understand what it's like to want to keep secrets."

"..."

"Eliot? You there?"

"You're, like, a Jedi master or something, aren't you?"

"Huh?"

"Now that you're not making me tell you, all I want to do is tell you."

"Ha. Then tell me! Honestly, if you're gonna try telling somebody, doesn't it make sense to tell someone who's on the outside fringe of your life?"

"Right . . . right, okay. Well, it's called *Lotus*."

"Hold on. Gimme a sec . . . Is your author alias Lettermaze?"

"Yup. Did you find it?"

"Holy CRAP. Eliot, the artwork is gorgeous."

"Thanks."

"And you have . . . TWENTY-EIGHT THOUSAND subscribed readers on Digitoons? Look at these comments. Holy CRAP, people love this comic. Wow, you even keep up an Instagram account for it, too?"

"Yeah. It's the best way to keep people updated on when I'm going to drop the next chapters and stuff. I can't post as often as other authors because of my full-time job. So, instead of dropping chapters every Tuesday or something like that, I usually end up just posting like crazy on the IG account to let people know my schedule and then dropping the chapters whenever I have them. It probably stunts my readership a little bit to not regularly release on a set schedule, but I'm all about limits. I can't do more than I'm doing right now without quitting my job."

"You have sixteen thousand Instagram followers."

"Yeah. People like the artwork I post there. I post a lot of sketches and concept boards and stuff."

"You just posted. Is this the painting you were just working on?"

"Yeah."

"So, your comic is about two different worlds?"

"Yup. Our world, and then a parallel, flipped world that's accessible only from underneath the lotus flowers in this one pond. And only when the lotus flowers are in bloom. Some of the characters go back and forth and get stuck on the other side and stuff like that."

"This is so kickass. This is SO KICKASS."

"I like it. I love it, actually. Sometimes I wonder if I should just—"

"Shhhhhh."

"Huh?"

"I'm reading."

"Oh, God. Don't read it right now!"

"I'll call you back later."

"JD! No! Please don't hang up on me in order to read my webcomic. Seriously. I'll just spend the next couple hours completely stressing about what part you're on and what you think and don't do this to me! You're supposed to be helping me sleep, not stressing me the hell out!"

"All right. I'll just read it later. And I won't tell you when I do, so you won't have a panic attack."

"Thank you."

"This is seriously cool, though. How come you've never told anyone else?"

"I guess because at first it was just this little hobby and I didn't think it would become anything. I've always had all sorts of little projects that I start and stop, and there didn't seem to be a reason to tell anybody about it."

"You weren't sure you were gonna stick with it."

"Right."

"And then?"

"And then, when it started to gain popularity, I think I liked having it all to myself. I live a pretty . . . regimented life. And I think having this big secret made me feel more interesting or something. Like I'm capable of surprises."

"I get that."

"It's my superhero side."

"Excuse me?"

"It's a theory I have. That everybody is secretly Spider-Man in some aspect of their life. There's the Peter Parker side that we show everybody. Which is the side that makes public appearances and goes out to dinner and buys Christmas presents for his family. But the Spider-Man side cruises the city at night and makes out with people upside down in the rain and has all these friends and enemies and dramas that the people who know Peter Parker will never know about."

"That . . . actually makes sense to me. It's kind of badass. I've never thought about it that way before."

"Does my theory apply to you? Do you have a Spider-Man side?"

"Hm. Well, I guess if we're thinking about it that way, sometimes I feel like I'm way more Spider-Man than anything else."

"You do seem like a very private person."

"Not usually. I generally pride myself on being an open book. But lately things have just gotten really . . . complicated. Anyway, *you're* probably my Spider-Man side. No one knows that I'm anonymously chatting with a random dude every night."

"Bo-ring. Everybody chats with randos at night. It's the nineties."

"Is that right?"

"You've never chatted with a random before me? Then what the hell are you using your internet connection for?"

"Talking to people is too stimulating. I usually use the internet to find something that will put me to sleep."

"Ah. Of course. I forgot the whole reason we've found ourselves in this situation. We're hopeless insomniacs."

"Hey, have you ever talked to anybody about it?"

"About why I'm not sleeping?"

"Yeah. Like a doctor or a counselor or something?"

"No, actually. I haven't."

"Pride?"

"Um . . . not exactly. It's more like, I already know the reason I'm not sleeping, so going to a doctor or a counselor just seemed like a waste of time. It's just something I have to get over. It'll take a little time. That's all."

"So, you're taking the tough guy route, huh?"

"Ha. No. That's part of the problem, actually."

"What do you mean?"

"Well, this whole not-sleeping thing started because of a sort of traumatic experience I had two months ago. And let's just say I was the *opposite* of a tough guy."

"Do you . . . want to tell me about it?"

"Eh. Not to dangle it out there and then leave you hanging, but . . . I'll tell you about it at some point. I just . . . not tonight."

"Sure. I didn't mean to pry."

"Ha. Are you joking right now? You're the queen of prying. You just bribed me with twenty-five points so that you could pry to your heart's content!"

"There are lines I won't cross! I won't pry about important stuff. I was only prying before because I wanted you to admit you were painting a nude self-portrait."

"Okay, well, now it's my turn to pry."

"You can try."

"How come *you* don't sleep, JD?"

"Hmmm. Habit mostly, I think. You know that phrase you have to wake up pretty early in the morning to whatever whatever?"

"Sure."

"Well, that phrase applies to my dad in a *literal* way. If I ever wanted to help him out with anything, I had to wake up pretty early in the morning. Or else he'd just already have done everything himself. So, at some point, I started going to bed after him and waking up before him."

"And your mom . . .?"

"Not in my life anymore."

"Ah. Sorry to hear that."

"It's okay, I guess. She was never a super-healthy presence in my life. It didn't take long after she left for me to realize that I just felt . . . kinda relieved? My dad has always made sure I felt loved."

"He really sounds like a great guy."

"He is. He's the best. That's why I . . . never mind."

"Hey, JD?"

"Yeah?"

"I'm doing my absolute best to mind my own business. But look, if you ever wanted to finish that sentence—doesn't have to be now—but I'll be here to listen to it."

"Thanks, Hoffman."

"You're welcome."

"So . . . ready to watch that baking show and hate ourselves for not buying any baked goods today?"

"I have no idea how something can possibly be so soothing and so torturous at the same time."

"Let's make a mental note to buy cookies tomorrow so we can be prepared for the torture tomorrow night."

"I cannot start eating cookies in bed every night, JD."

"Right. Gotta keep it tight for your nude self-portraits."

"You're obsessed with this idea. Now I know what I'm going to get you for your birthday."

"If you send me a nude self-portrait I will call the police."

"If I paint you a nude self-portrait I'll call the police on myself."

"Ha. Good to know."

"Hey, uh, I know we're joking around here. But just for the record, I'm not a perv."

"Um. Okay?"

"Like, I'm never going to do something like that."

"Like what?"

"Ah, send you a naked picture of myself."

"Oh."

"I just . . . I know that you don't know me very well, and I don't know you, like, at all. But I just wanted to be clear, in case you were worried about that at all. In the back of your mind or whatever. But I like you. I'd like us to keep talking. And I definitely don't want to traumatize you."

"I've seen you in person, Eliot. A naked picture of you would definitely not traumatize me."

"Hey—oh!"

"Wow, that really made your week, didn't it?"

"I may not know much about you, but at least I know you don't find me traumatizingly unattractive."

"You're incredibly easy to please."

"All it takes is a few compliments and a few imaginary points, and I'm good."

"I'll keep that in mind. All right. Baking show. Let's do this."

"I'm ready."

"Press play on the count of three?"

"One, two, three—bam."

Chapter Eight

"Hey, Eliot."

"Hi! You busy?"

"Nah. Just parking my bike real quick."

"Oh, are you out somewhere?"

"No. I'm just getting back. I was visiting my dad."

"You sound . . . sad."

". . . Seeing him can be really hard."

"Why? I thought you guys had an easy relationship."

"We do. I mean, he's pretty much my best friend. He's . . . the best. Like a grizzly bear. Except for with me and my brother. For us he's a total puppy. It's always sad to leave."

"Does he live in the city?"

"Yeah. Up in Queens. He's . . . sick. So he's living in a care facility. I'm taking care of things at home for him and going to see him as much as I can."

"Wow. God. That must be really hard. Is he—Does he—Will he—"

"Ever get better? No. It's terminal. He's not in a hospice facility yet. And I wanted to get an in-home nurse for him. But he sort of, um, works from home, and he didn't want his . . . clients . . . to see him failing in health. So he's up in Queens at an adult care facility right now."

"Oh, JD. God. I'm so sorry."

"Yeah."

"Are you . . . okay? I mean, that's probably a really dumb question to ask."

"No, it's nice, actually. No one really asks me that."

"Are you?"

"Yes. No. Sometimes."

"Oh, JD."

"Yeah. Sorry. I'm all right. Goofing around with you has been really nice. I should probably be focusing on other stuff. But, you're a really good distraction, Hoffman. It's been a while since I had fun."

"I am *extremely* glad to be of service. Like, over the moon, JD. Seriously. If fun is what you need right now, I will provide. I can think of like a hundred different things we—"

"Don't hurt yourself, Hoffman."

"Right, right. I'm going overboard, huh?"

"A tad."

"Okay. Got it. Be cool, Eliot. Be cool. Um, okay. New topic. What did you do today?"

"I worked."

"What's your work again?"

"You think you're soooooo slick, don't you?"

"Dang, thought I could sneak that one past you."

"I will not be telling you my job."

"Because your job is a dead giveaway?"

"Because my job is a dead giveaway."

"Interesting. Interesting. I'm filing away this information for future use. Hey. I've been thinking."

"Sounds risky."

"Do you want to meet my sister?"

"I . . . what?"

"Or talk to her on the phone? Or email with her or something?"

"I mean, she sounds cool from how you've described her, but . . . what are we talking about right now?"

"Or what about one of my clients? You could have their numbers. Or one of my buddies?"

"Eliot—"

"Or one of my neighbors? One of them is really chatty, but she would love to talk to you. Like it would make her year. She'd probably never let me forget it. But that'd be worth it, in the end, if it reassured you."

"Eliot—"

"Or my mom? I mean, obviously she's not very impartial but—"

"Eliot!"

"Yeah?"

"What are you talking about? Why do you want to introduce me to these people?"

"For character references."

"Why would I need character references?"

"Because you don't really know me. And you're obviously worried about getting to know me better. Probably because I'm mostly a stranger to you and men are generally terrible. But I thought that if you picked someone who knows me a little and asked them about me then you might have some reassurance that I'm not an axe murderer or a fuckboy or anything like that."

". . ."

"JD? You still there?"

"First off, I really love that you put axe murderer and fuckboy in the same category. Very astute."

"Just trying to, as the kids say, keep it real."

"Wow."

"Are the kids not saying that anymore?"

"*Anyway* . . . Secondly, I'm not scared of you, Eliot."

"Well, that's good. And you aren't, like, wary or suspicious of me, either?"

"No. I'm really not."

"Then . . . can I ask . . ."

"Yes. You can ask. Whatever it is."

"Are you hesitant to let me know who you are because you know me *too* well?"

"Huh?"

"Like maybe you already know that you don't want to meet in person because of the way I am? I mean, I know I'm a good person. But I definitely have some attributes that could be really, ah, frustrating to someone."

"Like what?"

"Like, I can be completely scatterbrained and thus make huge, messy mistakes."

"Really? Because it seems to me like you really have your shit together."

"Ha. Thanks. So then you definitely don't know me from before five or six years ago. Because back then, I was a total train wreck."

"I find that really hard to believe, Hoffman."

"I used to be really . . . disorganized."

"Well, you must have really gotten your act together because you come off as, like, the most organized person I've ever met in my life."

"Really? No way."

"Let's do a quick quiz to prove my point, okay?"

"Okay."

"What do you wear to meet with clients?"

"A suit, mostly."

"Anything in the front pocket?"

"You're trying to get me to admit to wearing a pocket square, aren't you?"

"If the penny loafer fits . . . Okay, how about on your coffee tables? What do you put under your drinks?"

"A coaster, obviously."

"How many coasters would you say you have in your house?"

"I don't want to say."

"Because the answer is incriminating?"

"Oh, fine. I have at least ten coasters that I can currently count from where I'm sitting."

"How about remote controls? Are they strewn around the room? Resting in a designated basket . . .?"

"Mmmmrrhphhprmrhr."

"What was that you're mumbling?"

"I said that I keep my remote controls arranged by size."

"Ha! See! I rest my case. You're a deeply organized person!"

"This is all because I've learned how to manage myself. After the fourth coffee table I ruined with drink rings, I realized that coasters were less expensive than new coffee tables. I dress up for business meetings because . . . well, it's like stage makeup, I guess. And it's ritualistic. I know that I need to be focused and aware and on my game when I'm doing work-related stuff, so I dress up in the whole nine. All the way down to the pocket square."

"Wow. Sounds like you make a lot of rules for yourself."

"I have to. Or else everything goes down the shitter."

"So, you've been living this lifestyle for five or six years?"

"Yup."

"What changed six years ago?"

"I . . . had something really embarrassing happen and realized that I needed to change things up."

"Oh, come on, Hoffman. You can't just leave a gem like that in the middle of the trail and expect me not to pick it up."

"What?"

"You had 'something really embarrassing happen'. You obviously have to tell me what it was."

"I . . . ugh."

"Well, why did you mention it, then!"

"No, no. I can tell you. I just need to adjust to the fact that you're going to fully see me as a cut-up from here on out."

"Hoffman, please refer once again to the number of pocket squares currently in your possession. You're clearly not a cut-up. You graduated college. You're good at your job. You keep in touch with your friends and family. I bet you jog, right? You strike me as a jogger."

"And once again, I can't tell if you're making fun of me or not."

"Just like God intended. But for real though, if you don't actually want to tell me, you don't have to."

"No, we can talk about it. I trust you. You're pretty much the least judgmental person I know, so . . . Well, I was well out of college at that point, working as a designer at this web company, living in Manhattan, basically fooling everyone in my life into thinking I totally had everything together. But, really, I was up to my ears in credit card debt and getting by at work through sheer talent, not hard work. I was stressed all the time. Lonely. When I met a new friend or a girl I was clicking with, it would only be a matter of weeks or months before I totally flaked on them and lost touch. But things really fell apart at my college friend's bachelor party in Vegas."

"Uh-oh."

"Yeah."

"You didn't . . . kill a stripper, did you?"

"What? Oh, my God! No. JD, if you would stay on the line with someone who would casually drop into conversation that they once murdered someone at a bachelor party then you really need to rethink your priorities."

"Point taken. So, what happened?"

"Well, his bachelor party included all of our friends from college, so there were both girls and guys there. And I had this one friend, Audrey, who I'd always had a crush on. And about a month and a half before the party, we started dating."

"Oh."

"Vegas was like the first official couple thing we did, and we were gonna tell all our friends we were dating. But . . . our first night there, we got really drunk and woke up the next morning with a marriage certificate on the nightstand."

"What?!"

"Yup. We got married. Like total idiots."

"Wow. I kinda thought that happened only in movies?"

"It happens in movies and to my dumb ass. Almost immediately our friends found out. Audrey and I were both mortified. I couldn't stop thinking about what would happen if my parents and my sister found out that I got married to someone I'd just started dating without them even being there. I mean, it's not like I want a white wedding or something, but if I were to ever do that for real, I'd at least want my family to be there."

"What happened with Audrey?"

"We got it annulled right away. But the whole thing was a complete headache and . . . getting a marriage annulled while you're trying to start a relationship with someone doesn't . . . work. It's like, part of the mystique of dating someone at the beginning is trying to see whether or not you have a future together. And by annulling the marriage, we were pretty much saying that no, we definitely didn't have a future together. It was like we were trying to start and end something at the same time. We didn't last more than a couple weeks post-Vegas."

"You . . . were really torn up about it?"

"I was really torn up about the fact that our friendship didn't survive. She didn't really want to talk to me any more after that, and honestly, I can't blame her. She was one of my closest friends for a long time and then everything just got so messy and now we're not even friends on Facebook. And I was torn up about how much the whole thing would have hurt my family if they'd ever found out."

"You didn't tell them?"

"No. I was too ashamed and raw over it. I just avoided the subject. Though I'm pretty sure they knew something was up. I'm a terrible liar."

"That must have been really hard."

"It was humiliating. And I was so angry at myself. The day my lawyer notified me that the marriage had been officially annulled I was sitting in my crappy little apartment I could barely afford and I looked around and all I could see were the dishes in the sink and the crumpled-up clothes on the floor. I just thought, *Eliot, it's now or literally never.* You know? Things had to change immediately or else I knew I was going to be having that same rock-bottom feeling again in a couple months or a couple years and I never wanted to feel like that again."

"So, you started organizing your life?"

"Yeah. I got a therapist and she kind of saved my life. She helped me figure out how to make my life work. Everything in its right place. So, now, here I am. Eliot 2.0."

"I like Eliot 2.0. A lot."

"Thanks. I do, too."

"But, to be honest, I probably would have been way more into Eliot 1.0."

"Hahaha. *What?!* How could you say that? You're ice-cold, JD."

"No! No offense intended at all."

"How could that *not* be offensive?"

"I wasn't trying to insult the person you are right now, I was trying to explain a fault of my own."

"Which is . . ."

"I'm pathologically attracted to men who don't have their shit together at all."

"Ah."

"Like, if 'accidentally got married in Vegas' was on some dude's dating profile, I'd be like, ooh, I'm intrigued."

"Oh, no. JD. *Standards.* You gotta have 'em."

"I'm learning that the hard way unfortunately."

"By dating a bunch of losers?"

"I hate to admit that I have to assign you ten points for accuracy."

"You use dating websites?"

"No, I don't actually. I don't have anything against them, but I prefer to meet dudes the old-fashioned way."

"Bars?"

"Monster truck rallies."

"Hahahahaa. Wait, for real?"

"I guess you'll never know."

"Gosh, I hope it's true. That's way cooler than how I meet women."

"Bars?"

"Yeah and online."

"Which works better?"

"Well, I'm not married or in a relationship so I'd say they are both equally shitty."

"Is . . . that your goal? To be married or in a relationship?"

"I mean, I'd rather be single than be in a *bad* marriage or relationship. But yeah. I'm thirty-six. I'd like to meet someone. Have a partner. Have a family."

"That's very . . ."

"That's very what?"

"I don't know. It's very *something*."

"Is that a good thing or a bad thing?"

"Oh . . . good thing."

"What about you? You're not looking for anything serious?"

"I'm in kind of a strange situation. It's not really conducive to being in a relationship."

"What do you mean?"

"Well, I've got my dad, who I'm kind of taking care of. And then I've got my brother, who I'm also always kind of perpetually taking care of. So, the idea of adding a boyfriend to that, yeah, I'm at capacity for people I have to take care of."

"When you think 'boyfriend,' you automatically think of someone you have to take care of?"

"I—I guess I do?"

"Good boyfriends help take care of you right back, you know."

"Do those men actually exist?"

"Definitively, yes. They do."

"Based on personal experience, I'm not convinced they do. Everyone I've ever dated either couldn't care less if I'm around or they need me to hold their hand through every moment of their lives. There is no in between."

"I mean, sure, men are the worst. No doubt. But not all of us are like that! And why would you date someone who couldn't care less if you were around?"

"I was young. And, I don't know, grateful to be involved with anybody."

"Grateful to be involved with someone who didn't care about you?"

"Let's just say that I didn't have a ton of interested parties in line when I was growing up."

"Awkward phase?"

"Took me a long time to grow into my nose. And find my style. And just generally figure out who I was."

"So then, once you did, you started meeting guys who were too dependent on you?"

"Yeah. It's kind of funny. Once I realized how badass I am, guys started being really interested in me. I guess you could say that I'm . . . someone who gets shit done? It's hard to explain. If there's something that needs to happen, I do it. For instance, when I got home yesterday, the light in my fridge was out. So, I turned back around, went to the hardware store, bought a new one, and installed it. If it's dinnertime, I make dinner. If it's time to change the sheets, I change them. And somehow that has translated into me being extremely attractive to men who don't know how to make dinner or change the sheets."

"Or who are willing to live with a dark fridge because that's easier than changing the light bulb."

"Bingo."

"Which is why you say you don't have enough time to date. Because you'll end up holding some grown man's hand so he doesn't get hit by a car while he crosses the street."

"Bingo again. Ten points."

"Oy. That's bleak. You know, it's kind of funny that this is the first time we're really talking about dating preferences."

"Why?"

"Well . . . never mind."

"No, really, why is it funny?"

"I guess just because we've talked about pretty much everything else."

"Not . . . everything, Eliot."

". . . Right. Do you think we'll get there, JD?"

"I hope so. I really do."

Chapter Nine

Jessie

I spend the next day catching up on work for Pops. Being at other people's beck and call is not my idea of a good time, but he passed this job over to me when I moved down here three months ago. We need the money and the apartment comes with the job so when he proposed I suck up my pride and take over for him, I didn't have a good reason to say no. The fact that he has come to really care for these people unfortunately also really matters to me. Because most of them I'd like to kindly request that they jump up their own asses. But for Pops, I answer their calls and run errands and do menial chores all day everyday. Because that's what he'd be doing if he was here.

In my old life, Saturdays used to mean something. I was an office manager at an education-based nonprofit in midtown, and I was good at it. To just look at me, you might not be able to immediately picture me in a collared shirt and tailored slacks, but that was me. Buttoned up and ready for work. My coworkers were scared of me just enough to not come to me with trivial problems. But whenever they did need something to be fixed or solved, I attacked the problem ruthlessly. The office was always immaculately organized. Every piece of mail catalogued, every broken-down desktop computer retired and replaced, old food in the fridge, gone without a trace.

And then the weekend would roll around, and it was almost like the office absolutely ceased to exist. I'd cruise around Queens on my bike. Go to concerts, go on dates, go to bars. I'd work out at my old boxing gym and head down to Brooklyn to make dinner for Pops while we watched the Yanks or the Knicks, depending on what season it was. I wouldn't even glance at the half of my closet that housed my work clothes. Weekends were when my real self emerged from the chrysalis for a glorious forty-eight-hour stretch.

But I quit that job when Pops got too sick to keep up with his work. We made the same amount of money, but with his free apartment in the mix, it only made sense for me to quit paying rent on mine and move down here to take everything over for him. And now, my weekends mean literally nothing. Because there's nothing these people won't ask me to do.

But at nine o'clock on Saturday night, I finally draw the line. Anyone who calls me now is going to get my voicemail until at least 10 a.m. tomorrow. I need to blow off some steam. I take a shower and even blow-dry my hair. I put on my *I mean business* lipstick. And decide that, yup, tonight is the night for my single pair of tight jeans. I slap on a sports bra and a tank top because, blow-dried hair be damned, I'm still me. And I'm out. Into the chilly spring night and practically jogging through Brooklyn to get where I'm going.

"Hey, Eliot."

"Remember the other night when you were giving me a list of things that you do when you can't sleep?"

"Yeah?"

"And one of those things was a pedicure."

"Uh-huh?"

"Well, how does one do that?"

"Do what? Give themselves a pedicure?"

"Yeah."

"You're gonna give yourself a pedicure?"

"Obvi."

"Oh. Well, you need stuff. Stuff you probably don't have around your house."

"I figured. I'm at the drugstore right now."

"To buy pedicure stuff?"

"To buy pedicure stuff. Are you all right? You sound like you're having trouble hearing me or something."

"No, I can hear you, I just . . . didn't know that men gave themselves pedicures."

"Well, I never have before, but I'm clearly open to the idea. Sounds kind of nice, actually."

"Okay, well, are you in the drugstore on Vanderbilt? Around the corner from the church."

"Yeah . . .?"

"Well, go to . . . I think it's aisle five or six. They have these, like, pedicure kits. It'll have everything you need."

"Hey, JD?"

"Yeah?"

"How the hell did you know which pharmacy I was in?"

"Oh. Shit."

"Is this where I find out that you've implanted a GPS tracker up my nose while I was sleeping?"

"No! Oh, my God."

"You hacked my phone and have been reading all my titillating work emails?"

"No! Eliot. No, it's nothing like that."

"Are you some all-knowing being? A poltergeist or

something? Oh, crap, is this like *The Sixth Sense*? Am I about to find out that you've been dead the whole time?"

"How could you joke at a time like this?"

"A time like what?"

"You're not freaked out in the least that I guessed which drugstore you were in?"

"All right, hold on. First off, is there a difference between the expensive pedicure kit and the cheap one?"

"If you're gonna use it more than once, get the expensive one."

"Great. Hold on, let me check out."

". . ."

"*Thanks, appreciate it. Have a good day!* Okay, JD. I'm back. And no. I'm not freaked out."

"How is that possible? You should be, like, calling the police right now!"

"JD, I'm gonna go ahead and assume that we know one another from the neighborhood, yeah? Either you live here or you work here, and since you know which neighborhood *I* live in, you were just taking an educated guess that I was at the one drugstore in walking distance. Right?"

"Yes. That's right."

"See? That's not scary at all. I'm sorry I made jokes about you stalking me. I obviously don't feel like you're stalking me."

"You swear you're not freaked out?"

"I'm not freaked out."

"I just can't help but think about if this were reversed. If you were the one who wasn't telling me who you were and you suddenly happened to know my exact location. I'd . . ."

"Report me?"

"Probably. I'd block your phone calls at the very least. And I'd check the expiration date on my mace."

"Well, the situation is not reversed. It's you and me, and I'm not scared of you, JD. If anything, you're keeping this whole secret because you want privacy from me, not because you're trying to butt into my life. In fact, I wish you wanted to meet me *more*. That way I could find out who you were."

"You don't think I'm . . . creepy?"

"You're allowed to have secrets, JD. Spider-Man, remember? I don't think of that as creepy. Especially because I'm a man who lives in your neighborhood and up until recently was pretty much a complete stranger. I get why you might be cautious about revealing personal information to me. I'm not entitled to your identity just because we've been talking on the phone."

"Eliot . . . that's not why I'm not telling you. It's not because I don't trust you yet."

"Then why is it?"

". . . It's complicated."

"Well, tell me later sometime. After you figure out that I really like you and I really like complicated stories."

"I . . . you're so . . . frustrating sometimes."

"Me? How?"

"You keep getting me all . . ."

"Getting you all what?"

"Nothing."

"What? Lay it on me. Why am I frustrating? What am I doing to you?"

"I take it back. You're not frustrating. At least not intentionally. It's my fault, really."

"If you explained it to me, maybe I could help figure it out."

"Just . . . never mind. It's not a big deal . . . You're gonna go do your pedicure now?"

"Yeah, I was hoping you could tell me how to do it."

"As much as I'd love to talk you through cutting your toenails, I'm actually out tonight."

"Oh. Wait . . . really?"

"Don't sound so shocked."

"I *am* shocked. You're a person who . . . goes out?"

"Oh, my God. Rude."

"No! I don't mean that you're, like, a recluse or something. But we've been talking every night for, I don't know, a while, and you've never gone out."

"It's only been four nights, Eliot."

"Wait. That can't be right."

"It is. It was just Tuesday that we talked for the first time."

"Wow."

"Yeah."

"We've really covered some ground in four nights."

"I know."

"So, now it's a Friday night and you're bailing on pedicures just so you can do something boring like go out in New York City?"

"Indeed."

"Where are you going?"

". . . To a club."

". . ."

"What's with the pointed pause?"

"Nothing. It's just, I'm learning that . . . you are someone who goes to clubs."

"So?"

"I'm just . . . recalibrating."

"Oh, my God. Are you judging me right now?"

"Absolutely not. Like I said, I'm recalibrating. No! I'm *integrating* this brand-new information about you . . . How often do you go to the club?"

"Maybe once every month or two."

"And what do you do there?"

"Drink. Dance. Stuff."

"Stuff?"

"I knew you were going to fixate on the stuff."

"JD . . . are you telling me that you go to the club to hook up?"

"*Eliot.*"

"Right! Right! It's none of my business. Sorry, sorry, I'll butt out. Man, I haven't been to a club in years. I kind of forgot that people still did that."

"Yes, Old Man River, people still go to clubs."

"I'm learning so much about you tonight, JD."

"Apparently I'm an open book right now."

"Okay, then. What's your name?"

"Minus ten points for stupid questions."

"Dang! Fair enough. So, you sound like you're outside. Are you already on your way to the club?"

"Yeah. I'm almost there now. Just a block away."

"Wait, you walked there?"

"Yeah."

"And I just learned that we know each other from my neighborhood. And there's only one real club around here. So . . . hold up. Are you going to Lights Out?"

"No comment."

"Oh, my God! You are! You're going to Lights Out. I haven't been there in years."

"Eliot?"

"Yeah?"

"Why do I feel like you're about to tell me that you're going to come?"

"I mean . . . am I specifically *not* invited?"

"It's a free country. I can't tell you not to come."

"Yes, you could."

"Huh?"

"I know I'm pushy, but if you actually don't want me to come, of course I won't."

"If you come, I'm not going to show you who I am, Eliot."

"But I might recognize you."

"It's a crowded club. There's no way you'd see me if I didn't want you to."

"Well, that's fine! That's cool! I'll come and just see the club! Like I said, I haven't been there in years. I just want to see the vibe. I want to see what you do on a Friday night every month or so. I won't look around for you, I promise."

"Do people ever say no to you, Eliot?"

"All the time. You should meet my sister. She derives great joy from shutting me down. It's like, her favorite pastime."

"I'll keep that in mind. All right. I'm here. I'm going to hang up now."

"I'm dropping the pedicure thingy off in my apartment and then I'll run over. Be there in twenty or so."

"Eliot."

"Yeah?"

"I meant it when I said that we're not going to see each other tonight."

"I know. I won't get my hopes up."

Chapter Ten

Jessie

This club has two floors and as soon as I get inside and get a beer I practically run to the second-floor balcony where I can watch the front door. I need to know the second he gets here. I wasn't lying, this club is packed with people, but if he was really looking for someone he recognized, he would probably spot me. I'll have to keep an eye on him so that he can't get an eye on me.

This club is the only one within walking distance of our neighborhood and because of that, anyone who wants to dance always kind of finds their way here. It has a reputation for decent music and healthy pours at the bar so everyone from fratty trust-fund babies to people who grew up in the neighborhood come here.

I don't necessarily stand out. But Eliot? I swallow my beer the wrong way as I spot him coming in the front door. He definitely stands out. He's in an expensive-looking sweatshirt and limited edition sneakers. His blondish hair reflects the blue and green lights from the dance floor. He looks like he's wearing a crown of sapphires.

I cover the bottom half of my face with my palm. My smile burns against my skin. His eyes trace around the room, and

I shrink back behind my new best friend, pillar. But then something interesting happens. Halfway through looking around the room, he freezes and drops his eyes to the floor. He scratches the back of his neck and makes his way over to the bar with his eyes cast down.

He's . . . intentionally not looking for me. Because he said he wouldn't.

My stupid inner-crush chokes on her popcorn. I have to duct-tape her hands behind her back before she starts doing the YMCA to get his attention.

Out of the corner of my eye I see a man approaching me. I turn. He's got two beers in his hands and a cocky smile. The blue-green lights reflect off his eyebrow ring and two lip piercings. His head is shaved and there are words spelled out on his knuckles. He eyes me up and down and looks like he's hit the jackpot. He probably thinks we're soulmates.

He opens his mouth to speak and holds the beer out to me.

"No," I say. "Thanks."

He frowns and opens his mouth again, once more holding the beer out.

"Hard no," I say.

His frown cements into place, and he opens his mouth one more time.

"Zero wiggle room," I tell him. "None."

He turns on his heel and disappears back into the crowd. By the time I'm peeking out from behind the pillar again, I've lost track of Eliot.

Panic closes a hand around my throat. Immediately, I'm scanning the second floor of the bar, looking for that golden head of hair, certain I'm about to see him staring at me from two feet away, his mouth dropped open as he realizes who I am, his bubble gum plopped on the floor.

It's fifteen terrifying seconds before I spot him on the edge of the dance floor down below, drink in one hand and his cell phone in the other. His face is screwed up tight as he scrolls through it. He looks like he's struggling to see it. Maybe his eyesight is bad?

Then his expression eases and his face lights up in triumph as he presses something on the screen and then holds the phone to his ear.

My pocket buzzes and embarrassingly enough, I actually squawk in surprise. He's calling me. I press a hand over my pocket and just watch him for a second. This is what he looks like when he's calling me. He gets that specific expression on his face. He bounces on his toes. He pulls his lips into his mouth.

Is he nervous?

Not once in all the hours we've spent talking did it occur to me that I might make him nervous at all. I really assumed that that was a one-way street.

I slip my phone out of my pocket and I'm about to answer it when a woman pulls apart from the crowd and approaches Eliot.

She's short, with pretty black hair and a big smile. He leans forward and looks intently at her face for a moment.

I know in that moment, instantly, completely, that he's trying to figure out if she's me. I'm gripping my beer so tight my fingers ache. I realize I'm leaning out from behind the pillar way too far.

Eliot leans back and says something to the woman. He shakes his head politely and gestures to his cell phone. But she's got the sleeve of his sweatshirt pinched between her fingers and she's yanking him onto the dance floor.

He looks adorably flustered, stumbling after her and trying not to spill his drink. He glances around the room before he quickly drops his eyes again. I smile behind my hand. Even right now he's trying to keep his promise to me.

The woman is a good dancer and is doing her best to get Eliot involved. Suddenly her ass is jammed against his crotch and his eyes get very big. He's lifting his drink high, trying not to spill it on her hair. She's shouting to a friend, and then, yup, magically there's a tallish brunette pressed against Eliot's back. Eliot sandwich. I shout with laughter at his expression. He tips his head back toward the woman behind him, and as the light catches on his face, I make an attempt to read his lips.

I'm Eliot, I'm pretty sure he just said to her.

I'm laughing hard behind my hand. He just introduced himself on the dance floor to the woman trying to freak him into next Tuesday.

He's too cute. This is terrible.

This is wonderful.

Everything in my life has become so much harder since he voice-messaged me the other night.

I finish my beer and then pass my phone from one hand to the other. Should I call him? Oh, who am I kidding, I pressed the call button ten seconds ago. The phone is already jammed tight to my ear.

He's still got his phone clutched in one hand, and down below on the dance floor he stops for a second while he squints at the screen. His face lights up, and he answers it.

"JD!"

"Well, you certainly didn't waste any time."

"You can see me?"

"Yup. And your dance partners."

"About that. I kinda didn't have a choice?"

"I saw."

"No chance of a rescue mission for me, huh?"

"None. I'm having too much fun."

"That makes one of us."

"Eliot, you might be too flustered to realize this, but you're dancing, too."

"Well, it's kind of hard not to when . . . look, I'm not exactly the one in charge of my hips right now. Stop laughing!"

"I can't! This is too good."

"I'm glad I amuse you."

"*What? Oh, sorry. No, thanks. Yeah. No, seriously. Yeah, I'm here with someone. Seriously, man, I'm not going to drink that. You might as well take it with you.* Eliot? You still there? Sorry about that."

"What was that?"

"Just some guy."

"Making the moves on ya?"

"I guess."

"Hey, JD?"

"Yeah?"

"Am *I* the person you're here with?"

"Huh?"

"You told him that you were here with someone. Am I crashing a date you're on right now? Or am I the person you're here with?"

"No comment."

"That means it's me, right? Cool, cool. Got it."

"Uh-oh. Sorry. Looks like you lost your dance partners."

"Yeah. I think disinterestedly dancing while on the phone with someone else wasn't doing it for them."

"Sorry."

"Don't be. Hey, JD, I have an idea."

"What's that?"

"Wanna dance with me?"

"Oh, my God, Eliot, how many times do I have to—"

"No, I mean, you don't have to show me who you are. Just maybe we could dance at the same time? You can be anywhere on the dance floor. I don't care. But, like, let's dance?"

"You're kind of a manic pixie dream girl, you know that?"

"Can I take that as a compliment?"

"I'm not the boss of you. You can take it however you want."

"Good. Are you on the dance floor yet?"

"Maybe."

"Can you see me?"

"Yeah."

"Cool. I might be Old Man River, but I've still got some moves, right?"

"You are . . . definitely cutting a rug."

"You were wrong about me being a manic pixie dream girl. If I were, I'd be dancing like this."

"Oh, my God! Stop that!"

"Yeah, wow. That's hazardous. I'm getting dirty looks."

"Probably because you're the weirdo flailing on the dance floor while he talks on his cell phone."

"And you're not?"

"I don't flail."

"Yeah, you're too cool to flail."

"How do you know that?"

"Because of the way you sound. It's pretty clear that you're cool."

"I do all right."

"That's what someone cool would say."

And so we do this. For almost an hour. He's staying on his side of the dance floor like a good little boy. And I stay on mine like a terrified little girl. I keep my back to him because I'm continually petrified that he's going to glance up and recognize me. And if he sees me, I won't be able to play it off. I'll have the phone to my ear and the look on my face to prove it.

Weirdly, it might be the most fun I've had on a dance floor in years. I'm alone but not alone and it . . . feels good. Eliot is in my ear and across the dance floor and it's just the two of us surrounded by extras in our movie. It's like we hired all these sweaty, horny, fun-loving people to hit on the downbeat. If I happen to glance at him during a random time, his dance moves are cute and kind of conservative. But if he's saying something to me and he thinks I might be watching, suddenly he becomes your dad at a cousin's wedding. He's trying to make me laugh, and it's working.

Because I have these things called boobs and I'm on a dance floor, it's inevitable that I have to deal with some suitors. Most of them back away quickly after making eye contact with me. I'm pretty sure my face says *Ruin this moment for me, and you're getting an elbow to the throat.* But a few of them are a little more persistent, and I have to work my way through the crowd to get rid of them.

A few times I'm suddenly too close to Eliot. I have to dog-collar my crush to keep her a safe distance away from him.

On my way out, I pass just two feet behind his back, close enough to see the way the sweat has curled the hair behind his ears. I'm playing with fire and I almost don't care. I'm torn between sprinting from the club and trying to suck that sweatshirt off him with a straw.

I'm five blocks away when Eliot realizes that something is different.

"Hey! Wait! I can't hear the bass on your end of the phone call. Did you leave?"

"Yeah. Sorry."

"Well, why didn't you tell me?"

"You seemed like you were having a good time."

"JD, you were the main ingredient to that good time. I do not need to stay in that loud, stinky club without you."

"Are you headed home now, too?"

"Yup. Ahh, fresh air. Well. *That* was an experience."

"Hey, can I ask you something?"

"Sure. Anything. I love this game. Ask me a million questions."

"Wow. Are you drunk off that one mixed drink?"

"I'm riding the high off my first club experience in half a decade. I feel like I could bench-press a car. I might never sleep again."

"God, you're like a kid after recess. I bet fifty bucks that you pass out the minute your head hits the bed tonight."

"Is that why you do this? Go to the club? You sleep well afterward?"

"Hey, I was the one who was asking questions, remember?"

"Right. Sorry. I got sidetracked. What was your question? Ask away."

"Do you have bad vision?"

"Huh? Oh, no. Twenty-twenty the last time I got an eye exam. Why?"

"Well, when I saw you looking at your phone earlier, you were squinting really hard, and I just wondered."

"Oh. Right. That."

"Sorry, is it something I shouldn't ask about?"

"No, no, that's fine. My vision is good but . . . I have trouble reading. So, sometimes doing stuff on my phone can be kind of a nightmare for me."

"Oh. Like dyslexia?"

"Bingo. And some other learning disorder-related stuff."

"Is that why you voice-message instead of text?"

"Yup. And I've found a lot of other strategies to manage it. But sometimes, when you're in a dark club with flashy lights and you can't voice-activate your phone, you just have to squint like an old man and try to decipher your contact list."

"Ah. I understand."

"It's funny."

"What is?"

"Well, I'm not ashamed of it anymore. I used to be terrified of someone finding out about it and I went to all these lengths to hide it, but over the years I've really come to terms with who I am. But, yeah, right now I'm learning that apparently I can still be a little embarrassed when I'm telling a pretty girl about it. It's surprising, is all."

"We've all got our stuff, Eliot."

"You too?"

"Oh, I definitely have my stuff. I'd tell you that you have nothing to be embarrassed about, but it sounds like you already know that."

"Yeah. Sometimes you just have to let embarrassment run its course, I think. That's the only way to get rid of it."

"True. Hey. Why'd you assume I'm pretty?"

"Oh. You had to turn down a few people at the club. I just figured you're probably cute."

"Ha. Wow. Cute is . . . not it. And honestly? I could be wearing a Charlie Brown pillowcase over my head and still get hit on at the club."

"Ah. I get it. So, you must be stacked, then."

"I—"

"Oh, my God, can we please go back in time and space to a dimension where I didn't say that? Jesus, Eliot. NO! Go back!"

"You sound like you're attempting to perform a magic spell right now."

"I'm waving my hands through the air like a wizard. People are crossing the street to get away from me."

"There goes your inner manic pixie dream girl again."

"Seriously though, I wish I hadn't said that. Did it offend you?"

"Eliot, do I sound like it offended me?"

"No. You sound . . . hey, JD?"

"Yeah?"

"Now can I ask you something?"

"Sure."

"You know how you aren't telling me who you are?"

"I'm familiar, yes."

"Well, is it a game to you? Because it's fun? Or . . . is there a real reason?"

". . ."

"I only ask because, well, for one, I really wanna know. But also because hiding who you are really doesn't seem like your style. Admittedly we don't know one another very well yet. But your vibe is somebody who is really confident in who you are. It just doesn't really fit this whole hiding thing."

". . . Hey, I just got back to my place. I'm gonna try to get some shuteye."

"Oh. Sure. Yeah. Of course."

"Talk to you later, Eliot."

"You too, JD. Hey! Wait!"

"Yeah?"

"I had fun tonight."

"Me too."

Chapter Eleven

Eliot

It's the morning after the club and I wake up to someone knocking on my front door. I peer at the sunlight dappling my bedspread through bleary eyes. As I stumble past the hallway mirror I see that my hair looks like someone tried to hide Easter eggs in it. I'm a disoriented cartoon version of myself as I swing open the door, complete with little boinging spirals of confusion springing away from my head.

My best friend, Fred, stands on my welcome mat looking equally confused. "Did I . . . get the day mixed up or something? We said Saturday, right?"

"Oh. Right. The thing. The thing. That thing we said we'd do." I'm snapping my fingers, trying to get my brain back online, meanwhile, Fred is cocking his head to one side and studying me.

"Late night?"

"Yeah. Sort of. What time is it? I must have slept in."

"It's ten."

"What? Wow. I slept for like six straight hours."

"You sound surprised. Have you not been sleeping well lately?"

"Yeah. No."

I'm beckoning Fred inside, pointing him toward the coffee maker.

I disappear for a minute. Wash up and pull some decent clothes on and then I'm back in the kitchen and Fred is pouring me a cup of coffee he's just brewed and orange juice for himself.

"Thanks, man."

"Is everything all right, Eliot?" Fred has these all-seeing eyes, and they're currently staring straight at me. He's an interesting guy. He set up his own internet startup a few years ago and it's really beginning to gain some traction. He's a computer genius, calm, kind, intuitive. But he's also reclusive and private and gets lost in his own world more often than not. It took me about a year to convince him that we should be best friends.

"Yes. Yeah." I don't tell him that I'm not sleeping well. Because then I might have to explain to him *why* I'm not sleeping well. And I haven't told anyone about that night. Not Fred. Not my family. "I'm just a little disoriented is all. I went to a club last night."

He chokes on his orange juice. "What? A club? Why?"

Fred would volunteer to do someone else's taxes before he'd freely walk into a club. He's quiet and contemplative and not into sweating all over strange women. Which is one of the many reasons I really wish he'd just date my sister already. He's a stand-up guy and pretty much the opposite of everyone she's ever dated. I've been angling for years to set them up, but Vera has told me to shove my dating suggestions up my ass in about a thousand colorful ways, and Fred has become very adept at changing the subject. I wish they'd stop being stubborn and just meet one another already. I'm positive I'm right about them being a match.

"I had . . . kind of a date?" I tell him by way of an explanation for my first club experience in half a decade.

"Really? With who?"

I give him the short version. "With a wrong number I didn't mean to text. We've been talking a fair amount."

"So you decided to meet up with her at a club?" He still looks like he has absolutely no idea why anyone would ever do such a thing. I almost laugh at the expression on his face.

"Well, technically we *didn't* meet up."

He cocks his head and waits for me to explain.

"Because, technically, I don't know who she is."

His brow furrows but still he patiently waits for me to continue.

"Because, technically, she won't tell me who she is. Even though, technically, we've already met at some point before."

"So . . . you went to the club . . ." He shakes the cobwebs out of his head. "To meet a woman you simultaneously know and don't know. But you didn't meet up with her. And then you came home."

"Yup."

"Well . . . okay?"

I laugh. "I like her."

"Like, romantically?" He looks slightly unsure how to have this conversation. Fred doesn't often talk about romance.

"I think so? It's kind of hard to tell, since I don't know who she is."

"Right. That eensy-weensy detail."

"Here. The boxes are over here." I point him to the living room where I've boxed up a bunch of the old equipment I used to use in my graphic design job. I was employed by a big tech company for a while, that's actually where Fred and I met. The job was a little bit over my head when I started and I ended up buying a bunch of different tablets and mouses and touchscreens and all sorts of digital-age detritus that I thought would give me a leg up. Now that I work from home and I've figured out the best setup for myself, it's all just gathering dust. Fred volunteers at this afterschool program that teaches kids how to code, and I offered to donate the equipment. He said he'd come by today to see what they could and couldn't use.

He kneels down and starts pawing through the equipment. "This is great, Eliot. We probably wouldn't use this or this. But everything else is awesome."

"If we carry it down to my car, I can drive it over right now."

"Great!"

We're schlepping the boxes down the stairs, but my mind is still on JD. Apparently so is Fred's.

"So, is it that she doesn't want to tell you who she is, or she just doesn't want to meet up with you?"

"Um. I'm not sure. Maybe both? But she's definitely set on not telling me who she is."

"Huh."

"Any guesses why? It's kind of stumping me."

"Any guesses as to why a woman might not want to give out information involving her identity to a random dude she maybe kinda vaguely knows and has only had a few phone conversations with?"

"Yeah. You're totally right. To her, I could just be some strange perv."

"I mean, if she's met you then she probably knows you're not a total perv. You're a good person and that's pretty clear from the get-go. But even so, she might be . . . waiting? To get a better read on you? Or she might never want to tell you. Maybe anonymity is important to her for any number of reasons."

"Like what?" I ask as I lean to one side, attempting to open the front double doors of the building with one foot. They're sticky and not cooperating, so I lean my weight on one of the doors and kick my foot up higher on the other, heaving them open.

Fred, who like I said, is a genius in some ways, is not exactly a genius in others, and for reasons known only to him, instead of stepping over my extended leg, attempts to duck under it.

"Aaahahggghaahhh! Fred!" But it's no use, he's already halfway underneath me, clutching a box full of expensive equipment. I improvise, kicking my leg even farther up the doorframe and nearly tearing out the ass of my pants at the same time.

Of course, because it's been years since the universe allowed me to look cool, this is the exact second that my tatted-up super opens the door of her first-floor apartment. I look back over my shoulder at her as her eyes grow wide.

"Just. Trying. To. Move. Some. Boxes," I tell her, straining between each word because I'm pretty much doing the splits while my friend does the limbo.

She covers the bottom half of her face with her hands, but the damage is done. She's obviously laughing at us. At me. As usual.

She strides forward and holds the far door for me. My leg falls down and I try to shake some blood back into it. Nothing left to do but flee the scene of the crime.

"Thanks," I shout back over my shoulder to her as the doors to the building fall closed.

"What were you saying?" I ask Fred, hurrying to catch up to him.

"Oh. Just that people have all sorts of reasons for wanting to maintain anonymity. Think about the internet. People find a lot of freedom or comfort in being anonymous."

"Sure, but aren't people usually worse versions of themselves when they're anonymous? Like, so they can troll? And that's not JD at all. She's so sweet. Well, sweet isn't the right word for her. But she's got a ton of integrity. You can just tell. I'd be willing to bet that she's pretty much always the best version of herself, anonymous or not. That's just the vibe she gives off."

We're walking up to my car right now and I'm busy trying to dig my car keys out of my pocket and balance the box on one hip, so it takes a minute for me to register the look that Fred is giving me.

"JD?"

"Oh. That's what I call her."

"Hey, Eliot?"

"Yeah?"

"Never mind."

That's one of the things I like best about Fred. He doesn't ever feel the need to get the last word. If he were my mother, or even my sister, he wouldn't be able to restrain himself. The words would be written all over his face. He'd write it down and get it notarized. He'd call me again in half an hour to remind me. But Fred is Fred. So, instead, he just gives me a look, assumes I'm not an idiot, shuts his mouth, and the two of us drive to drop off the supplies.

Chapter Twelve

Jessie

I'm elbow-deep in tepid bathwater when my phone buzzes in my pocket. I immediately dry off and make a grab for it. It might be Pops and, yeah, it might be Eliot. It's the little things that are bringing me joy these days.

I frown at my phone because it's not a phone call, it's a text, and it wasn't who I was hoping it was from. It's from my cousin Tasha.

Need some backup, it reads.

I groan when I look at the picture attached to it. It's my brother, Jack, passed out on her living-room floor.

This is absolutely not what I need right now.

Be there in an hour, I text her back. I can't leave before I unclog this tub for my neighbor, Miss Cynthia, and Tasha's apartment is a few neighborhoods up in South Williamsburg so I'll need a little time.

She texts me back a thumbs-up and I send up a silent prayer of thanks that Tasha's living-room floor is the one that Jack picked to pass out on. We're not that close but she's always been really kind about the type of drama that seems to be written into Jack's DNA.

I finish snaking the drain and then quickly wash up.

"All done, honey?" Miss Cynthia asks as I walk through her kitchen.

"Yup, should be good."

She gestures toward a plate on the table in front of her. My payment for getting out of bed at 6:45 a.m. to fix her bathtub is a double-decker sandwich on toasted rye. Since I've moved in here, I've learned that her sandwiches absolutely kick ass. But that wasn't what had me answering the door this morning. It was knowing that Pops wouldn't have even made her knock twice. He'd have been answering the door on the first knock.

Gotta take care of the neighbors. How many times has he said this to me over the course of my life?

I've never lived anywhere but Queens or Kings County, and neither has Pops, but he's convinced that if you've never broken bread with the people next door, then you're not doing New York right.

After Mom left and our family unit went from four to three, Dad started taking extra care to connect with our neighborhood. I think he was under the impression that if we took care of them, they'd take care of us. And maybe he's on to something. Because Miss Cynthia's bathtub is in full working order again and I've got a breakfast sandwich to go.

It's a gorgeous spring morning, and I'd love nothing more than to take my bike up to Tasha's, but I'm assuming I'm going to have to drag my brother's drunk ass home. So, instead, I grab the keys to Pops's van and fight traffic north.

Forty minutes later Tasha answers her door with a grim little smile. The smile is for me. The grimness is for the state of my miserable brother.

"Dammit." I can't help but sigh when I see him. He's in the exact same position he was in in the picture Tasha sent me so

I'm assuming he hasn't moved at all for the last hour. "He passed out like that?"

"Yeah. He was absolutely blitzed when he showed up at my door."

"Why'd he come here?"

Any trace of a smile leaves her face now and she looks like she really doesn't want to tell me. Her lack of response gives me all the answer I need.

"He was hitting you up for money, wasn't he?"

She gives me a single nod.

Tasha runs a really popular relationship and sex advice podcast and has become something of a minor celebrity over the last few years. She's definitely our most successful family member, but it's not like she's rolling in it or anything.

"Tell me you didn't give him any."

"Of course not! Especially not while he was this drunk. If he still needs it when he sobers up then—"

"He doesn't, Tash. He doesn't need it. His job pays him more than enough for anything he could possibly need. And if he needs more, that means he pissed his paycheck away or he's working up some sort of scheme again. Don't give him any."

She chews her lip. "I was just wondering if your dad's care facility was putting some strain on you guys."

"It's not putting a strain on Jack." The words aren't bitter in my mouth. Just heavy with sadness.

"You're paying for all of it by yourself?"

I shrug, not wanting to get into it. "Pops is on Jack's insurance from work. So, as long as Jack keeps his job, then we've decided to call it even. We're all doing our part."

She looks like she wants to argue with me on that one, but Jack starts stirring and for the next fifteen minutes, he gets all of our attention while we drag him up off the floor.

I'm strong, and so is Tasha, but it is a holy miracle that we manage to schlep my ridiculous brother down the stairs of her walk-up and into the van. He's a groaning rag doll as I buckle him into the back seat. My muscles are burning, my toes are stubbed, I'm sweaty and frustrated, and tears start pricking at the back of my eyes.

"Tash, I'm so sor—"

"Don't apologize," she cuts me off, a hand on my shoulder. "If you apologize for his behavior, that means that you're taking some responsibility for it. And the only person who should be taking responsibility for it is this dumbass. When he sobers up, tell him he owes me an apology."

"I will."

She gives me a quick, tight hug and watches from the curb while we drive away. Tasha is good people.

It's after I've driven three blocks back toward Pops's apartment that I remember I can't, under any circumstances, bring Jack there. He burned that bridge to the ground. He can never go back there. Which means that I have no other choice but to bring him back to his place. Which means I'm gonna have to see . . .

"Dammit, Jack! You absolute asshole!" I pound once on the steering wheel and glare at him passed out in the backseat.

I make it to Jack's half an hour later and park up on the curb in front of his basement apartment in Queens. I pound on the door of his apartment, wanting nothing more than to get this over with as quickly as possible.

Trent, Jack's roommate, opens the door with no shirt on. Because apparently he's still allergic to shirts.

His eyes widen and then go sly when he sees it's me. "Hey, girl."

He thinks I'm here for him. I'd rather be scuba-diving through puke. I should probably mention that Trent is an ex-boyfriend. A recurring one. But the last time we broke up three years ago, I swore it was the last time, and it's stuck. I know he's just waiting for the day I come tap-dancing back to him, but see the aforementioned puke reference. It's never going to happen.

"Your roommate is passed out in my van. Come get him."

I turn on my heel and walk back to the van, yanking the sliding door open and unbuckling Jack. Trent appears at my side, stomping the back of his heels into some boots and tugging a tank top down. Tattoos cover almost every inch of his chest and arms, even more than when we were dating. At a glance, I can see two different girls' names that didn't used to be there. I don't check to see if he's still got my name on the opposite shoulder. I honestly couldn't care less.

To Trent's credit, he doesn't complain as he single-handedly heaves Jack into the house. I stand at the front door and watch as Jack crumples back onto the living-room couch with a groan. My work here is done.

"Thanks," I say to Trent, because I honestly couldn't have dragged Jack into the house by myself. "Later."

I'm at the driver's side door of the van when Trent catches up to me.

"Hey! Where are you going so fast? Stay for breakfast."

Unless he's undergone drastic changes in the last three years, breakfast is likely going to be rubbery scrambled eggs covered in ketchup. I point to Miss Cynthia's wrapped-up sandwich in my front seat. "I'm good."

"All right, stay for coffee, then."

"Trent, I'm really good." I slide into the front seat. When I roll down the window, he's standing there with his arms crossed just glowering at me.

"You should come around more," he tells me. "Your brother's been having a tough time."

I know that Trent's telling the truth, but he's always been good at telling the truth in the most painful way possible. He's honest, but not kind. That's probably why we were so drawn to one another back in the day. We used to have that in common. I, on the other hand, have been working on the kindness part these last three years.

"I'll call him this week." I start the van, but Trent puts one hand on the rolled-down window to keep me from driving away.

"He thinks you hate him."

That takes some of the wind out of my sails. I don't hate my brother. I could never. It's true that even before Eliot came into my life recently, I've been taking some steps back from Jack. I love him forever. But the man is draining. Frustration is boiling in my gut right now, and Trent is the very last person I want to be talking to. "That's ridiculous. I've just needed a break from his drama for a while."

I realize a second too late that I've said that very same sentence before about Trent himself. To his face. When we broke up.

His face pulls tight. "Sounds familiar."

"Yeah? Well, I'm sorry that it's true."

Trent steps back and lets the car go. He's shaking his head as I drive away. I've gotten the last word and I wish I hadn't. I didn't go there to fight with Trent. Especially because he's got this twisted idea that fighting is quote-unquote "our thing." He seems to think that whenever we fight with one another it's keeping our spark alive. In reality, it just exhausts me. And makes me sad. I'm friends with a few of my exes, and considering Trent is Jack's best friend, it would be nice if the two of us could be friends, too.

But I just don't see that happening. He's too combative. Too convinced that we'll get back together someday. And if I'm being honest, he's too mean. He's got his soft moments, but when he gets mad, truly mad, there's nothing he won't say to win an argument. I'm never going back there again.

As I'm driving, I switch off the radio and just think. Ever since I took over Pops's job, it's the rare moment when I get to just think. There's always someone calling me needing this or that, or I'm hauling ass up to his care facility to spend time with him. It's nice to just let my brain wander wherever it wants.

My crush taps a high heel against the floor and gaudily shuffles a deck of cards to get my attention. Of course my brain goes there. I can't help but think of Eliot. A ridiculous fantasy enters my brain. It's Thanksgiving, and I'm sitting at the table with Pops, Jack, and Trent, like we usually do. Only this time, there's another person at the table. Eliot is sitting next to me.

I almost laugh at the absurdity. I mean, Pops would like Eliot a lot. I'm sure of it. For starters, Pops likes anyone who's nice to me. But Pops especially likes people who are goofy, not too self-serious, easy-going. The way Jack used to be.

It would be fun to have Eliot and Pops in the same room. But what about Eliot and Trent?

"Ha." I can't help but say it out loud. Trent would burst a blood vessel if I brought clean-cut, beautiful, white-toothed, friendly-smiling, polite, generous, sweet Eliot around. When I'm talking to Eliot, it's like a fluffy white cloud surrounds me. I imagine having that Eliot cloud when Trent is near. Would it be like protective gear? Would it keep me from getting singed? I don't know him all that well, but I bet Eliot would love to be that person for somebody. He would love to be their cloud of protective happiness and support. It sounds like heaven.

My smile fades. Because I imagine the last combination of people: Eliot and Jack.

That's the one that no matter how I imagine it, will never work. They can never be in the same room together. Eliot can never figure out who my brother is.

I rest my head on the steering wheel at a stoplight.

If Jack hadn't done what he did, would I have already told Eliot who I am? Would we have already made plans to meet up? Would we have gone on a date? Kissed already?

Would I have a future with this guy I have such a monumental crush on?

I park the car back at Pops's apartment and pull out my phone. I go to Eliot's contact information and just look at it. My urge is to call him.

But I shouldn't. I know I shouldn't. There are only very small parts of Eliot Hoffman that I'll ever be allowed to have. And honestly, I should learn to be grateful for what I've got.

Chapter Thirteen

Eliot

The minute, no, the *second* I finish work, I'm up out of my chair and ripping at my dress shirt like I'm Clark Kent mid-transformation. I shrug into a sweatshirt and jeans and grab my keys and wallet. I have to get out of my apartment ASAP before I do something stupid. Like call JD thirty times in a row until she answers.

She hasn't called me since the night at the club and it's been a few days and I might be, ya know, starting to lose my marbles over it. I really, really don't want to push her, but I also really, really want to talk to her. So, I decide to take a stroll through my neighborhood in an attempt to control my baser urges. She'll call me when she wants to call me.

I'm three blocks from my building, hands in my pockets, when I back up a few steps and peek into the window of a Mexican restaurant I just passed by. I'm squinting at my sister hunched over the bar, pecking away at her phone with one hand and chewing on the fingernails of her other hand. We live in the same neighborhood, so I'm not completely shocked to see her, but it's always strange to unexpectedly observe someone you know out in the wild. For a moment, I see Vera through the eyes of a stranger. There are lines of worry on her face, lit blue by the glow of her phone, and there's a plate of tacos going ignored next to her. This . . . does not look healthy.

I head in, pull up the barstool next to her, and wait for her to notice me. Ten seconds pass and she's still typing on her phone. She's apparently done with the fingernails and has moved to pistoning one of her legs up and down a mile a minute. I reach over and take a bite of one of her tacos. She still doesn't notice. The bartender does notice though, and I mouth the word "sister" to him with a shrug and a roll of my eyes. He nods and smiles and pantomimes giving me a drink. I point at Vera's michelada, and within moments, I've got one of my own in front of me. There's only half a taco left when Vera finally looks up.

"Hey! *Hey!*" She looks like she's about to throat-punch the taco-stealer and then, when she realizes it's me, she looks like she's about to titty-twist the taco-stealer.

"At first I was just waiting to see how long it would take for you to notice me, but then the tacos were really good," I say with a shrug.

She mumbles something that I can almost guarantee involves a creative way of making me see stars and then motions to the bartender for another plate of tacos.

"You a little busy there?" I ask, motioning toward her phone. "You didn't notice I was here for like ten straight minutes."

And just like that, the obstinate, irritated expression on her face melts away and concern furrows her brow. "Yeah. I was emailing with one of the organizers of that expo I'm doing next week. And I guess I'm a little stressed about it."

"Stressed why? Are things getting messed up?"

She glares at me. "No, nothing is getting messed up. It's just a lot to coordinate and I want to make sure that everything is perfect."

"Sure." She's prickly, irritated again, and I'm not exactly sure why. "Look, if you need help with anything . . ."

"I don't need help," she says immediately. "I can do it on my own. I *am* doing it on my own."

"Okay," I acquiesce. Vera is normally a very easy person to get along with. She's funny and loose and open. But when it comes to her new business, a care package subscription service, she's tense and closed-off and, apparently, unwilling to accept help of any kind.

A minute of silence passes, both of us sipping our drinks, when finally, Vera sags at the shoulder and turns to me. "What if . . ." she starts. "What if, for once, you weren't the perfect one?"

Bubbly, salty, lime-y michelada goes up my nose, and for a moment, I think I might have done permanent damage to my . . . whatever you call those. My olfactory thingies. By the time I've finished getting the drink out of my nose, Vera is halfway through the tacos that have just been delivered to her and she seems to have regained some of her humor. She's peering at me with one raised eyebrow.

"You all right there?"

"Did you just refer to me as the perfect one?" I am seriously unsure if I heard her right.

"It's a shame there are only two of us," she says. "It's constantly a direct comparison. There's Mr. Perfect and Ms. Cut-Up. If we had another sibling, maybe there'd be some middle ground." She gets a dreamy expression on her face. "I'd love to live in the middle ground. Sounds like heaven."

I'm blinking at her, trying to process this line of thought. "You're referring to me as Mr. Perfect and you as Ms. Cut-Up?"

She fiddles with the decoratively cut radish on the side of

her plate. "I guess I'm just wondering what would happen if I . . . started doing better. If my business took off. You think there's room for both of us to be perfect? Or would one of us get bumped down automatically? You know . . ." She lowers her voice menacingly. "There can only be one."

I laugh, but it's only cursory. I kind of can't believe what I'm hearing right now. "Vera . . ."

Just then her phone buzzes in her hand, and she gets that line of concern between her brows again. "Shoot. It's the organizer. I hate to dine and dash, but . . ."

"Don't worry," I tell her. "Go ahead."

She reaches for cash in her purse but I frown and give her a playful shove toward the door. I'm not trying to be patronizing, but I'm her big brother and there are some things I like to do for her. I can buy my baby sister some tacos every once in a while.

She leaves, answering the phone as she gets onto the sidewalk, and I watch her go. I sit at the bar on my own for a long time.

Mr. Perfect.

A blooper reel of my own life is playing in my mind.

I laugh and shake my head. If only Vera knew.

Chapter Fourteen

"Hey! JD!"

"Hey, dude."

"How are you? How have you been? I didn't hear from you for a couple nights. I was starting to wonder if everything was all right."

"If you were worried, then why didn't you call me instead?"

"Well, I wondered if I'd pushed it too far with the club thing. I know that I can be kind of, I don't know, *intense*. And I wanted to give you some space. To make sure you didn't feel too pressed."

"Ah. No. That was fun. I didn't call the last couple nights because . . . I was busy with something else."

". . . You're just gonna let that dangle out there like that? You're not going to tell me what you were busy with?"

"I promised you I wouldn't mention it."

"Huh?"

"I'm saving you a panic attack."

"What? Oh! Oh, my God. You didn't call me the last few nights because you were busy reading my webcomic?"

"Bingo."

"Jeez. You mean to tell me I was getting cockblocked by my own artwork?"

"I—"

"Never mind. Strike that from the record. I didn't say that. I don't say things like that. Just forget it. God. Okay, well, what'd you think about the comic?"

"It's good."

". . ."

". . ."

"That's it? That's all you're going to say?"

"I like it."

"JD. I like you, but you're the absolute worst."

"What? What do you want me to say?"

"You're literally the only person in my life who knows I do this. Come on! Gas me up a little bit!"

"Okay. Um. You're good at making webcomics, Eliot."

"Wow. I've never felt so proud of myself before."

"If you want compliments, just read the comments section! People there can't wait to tell you you're a genius. What do you need me for?"

"Obviously your opinion matters to me more than anonymous internet readers."

"Well, I like the comic. What more do you want from me?"

"Nothing, nothing. I know you're not the most effusive person in the world. I'll just pretend you gave it a glowing review."

". . ."

". . ."

"So, like, what happens with Shaker after that cliffhanger? Does she make it back to her own world or . . .?"

"Oh. MY. GAWD."

"What?"

"You little scamp! You're not calling to check in with me about my life. You're calling to try and squeeze some spoilers out of me!"

"What? No way."

"So, I was wrong? You just happened to bring up that cliff-hanger in casual conversation? You couldn't care less what happens to Shaker?"

"I . . . okay, FINE. I'm totally obsessed with your stupid addictive webcomic and I'm freaking DYING to know what happens next and if you strand Shaker in that dumbass reverse universe I swear to God I'll strangle you myself."

"HAHAHAHAAAAAA YESSSSSSSSS. This is officially the best thing that has ever happened to me."

"Spill your secrets!"

"No way! You think I'd just tell you?"

"Eliot! Come on! I've done basically nothing but read this webcomic for eighty hours straight and I get to the last page and my favorite character might end up trapped in an alternate universe for all eternity? Which would be fine, if Hertzog were there with her and then they could just start their life afresh in a new place and I wouldn't care. But Hertzog is off doing that stupid boot camp for psychics thing—"

"Wait, does that mean that you're shipping Shaker and Hertzog together?"

"Of course! I am definitely not shipping Shaker and Rowan."

"That's who most of the readers ship."

"Rowan is such a little shit. He's too smooth for his own good, and besides, he had his shot when they were stuck in the time warp, but he blew it. Next. Move on. It's Hertzog's turn."

"I seriously cannot tell you how much joy this is bringing me. Whatever the opposite of a panic attack is, I'm currently having it. This is a euphoria attack. There's too much oxytocin in my bloodstream right now. I'm gonna pass out."

"You're not going to tell me anything, are you?"

"Do you really want me to? You actually want me to spoil it

for you? Whatever happens next, you don't want to see it in living color? You just want me to explain it in my regular old voice? If that's what you really want, I can spoil the whole rest of the series for you."

"Ugh. No. Fine. You're right, you butthead. I don't want you to spoil it. But I do want you to finish it and publish it immediately!"

"I was just working on it earlier today. Trust me, I'm putting as much time in as I possibly can."

"Remember how you said you'd have to quit your job in order to have enough time to post regularly?"

"Yeah."

"Well, I think that's a good idea. I think you should quit your job. In fact, I'll just go ahead and draft your letter of resignation for you right now. That'll make it easier."

"This is incredible. I could never have predicted this in a hundred million years. I can't believe you're my fangirl. I must have done something right in a past life."

"Can you get me a discount code on some of this merch? Friends and family or something? I want one of the T-shirts."

"Don't pay for the merch! I'll get it for you for free."

"Obviously I've blown my cover on how cool I think this all is. But really, I can't believe you do all of it on your own."

"Well, I don't do it completely on my own. There's a team that works on the color-blocking for me. Art and design students, mostly. Especially when I'm up against a deadline. And I have a story editor and two proofreaders who help me with the writing."

"Right. I wondered if your learning disorder stuff made that part difficult."

"I can voice-to-text most of it, but of course, that always ends up making all sorts of stupid mistakes. And anything I input myself is always spelled embarrassingly wrong. The proofreaders have their work cut out for them."

"The Spider-Man side of you is the coolest thing ever. And now I can definitely never tell you who I am."

"What?! Why?"

"Because there's nothing awesome like this hidden in my closets. My Spider-Man parts are just sad little family skeletons."

"I'll let you see the panels for the next five chapters early if you tell me who you are."

"Ugh . . . that's so not fair. You're cheating."

"I'm just playing all my cards. That's different than cheating."

"Eliot?"

"Yeah?"

"You're not dreaming that I'm secretly Gigi Hadid or something, right?"

"Gigi who?"

"She's a supermodel."

"You're asking if I'm assuming that you're secretly rich and famous?"

"I don't know. It's just this whole thing with us kind of lives in a fantasyland, and I'm wondering if somewhere in your mind you're also thinking of me as, you know, a fantasy."

"JD, considering I've never met any famous supermodels, I've definitely crossed that possibility off my list."

"Okay."

". . . I mean, are you asking what I picture when I imagine you?"

". . ."

". . ."

"I guess so."

"I picture a she-blob."

"I'm sorry?"

"Well, I don't know what you look like. So I just picture this, like, shadow person. Average height, average size. And sometimes when I'm bored, I add Marge Simpson hair."

"You're being serious right now?"

"Completely! And every morning before work I put you in a Camaro in my brain and send you off into the sunset so I don't spend the whole day trying to solve the mystery of who you are."

"If that webcomic weren't proof of how vivid your imagination was, I probably wouldn't believe this."

"Hey! That's a good idea. Hold on."

"What am I waiting for?"

"I'm going to draw what you look like in my head. And then I'll take a picture and send it to you."

"Didn't you just say that you picture me as a she-blob?"

"Kinda, yeah."

"Well, I'm pretty sure I can picture that already, but sure, knock yourself out."

"Keep talking to me while I draw."

"Okay."

". . ."

". . ."

"JD?"

"Yeah?"

"The important part of the sentence 'Keep talking to me while I draw' was the 'talking' part."

"Oh. Right. Um . . . what have you been up to over the past few days?"

"Well, tons of work. I just finished this big design project for my main client."

"Do you like being a freelancer?"

"I love it. I have to be my own boss. I liked the whole job security thing when I was on staff at my old company, but having to follow a bunch of someone else's—seemingly arbitrary—rules made the job about a gazillion times harder for me."

"I get that. I used to work in an office and I definitely felt like a lot of the company-wide policies were pretty infantilizing. It was like we couldn't be trusted not to burn the place down if we didn't sign the HR handbook when we got hired."

"Exactly."

"So, you worked over the last few days. And I'm assuming you put in many hours on your webcomic, otherwise I'm going to have a stroke."

"Yes. Deep breaths. I finished almost an entire chapter."

"Excellent. Did you do anything else?"

"I hung out with my sister yesterday after work."

"Vera, right?"

"Yeah . . . it was unplanned. I just happened to run into her at a restaurant we both like."

"How'd it go? You sound a little weird about it."

"Well, she said something that's been bothering me, actually. Where do I start? Okay. Well, she's got this big expo thing coming up in a few weeks, and I've been helping her plan parts of it out."

"She's running the expo?"

"No, no. She's a participating vendor for her care package subscription service. It's really cool. And her business is just starting to take off. I'm really proud of her. But last night it seemed like she was really struggling with some of the organizational parts of it, and I offered to help her."

"Uh-huh."

"Well, she was, like, mortally offended that I'd offered to help, and then she called me Mr. Perfect and herself Ms. Cut-Up. And then I literally choked on my drink."

"Because you don't think those labels are accurate?"

"Are you kidding? Do I need to tell you the Vegas story again? I'm the biggest cut-up there is. I could win the Cut-Up Olympics."

"Yeah, well, Vera doesn't know that story, does she?"

". . . No. I kept it from everybody."

"So, all she knows is that you're this successful, well-oiled machine, right?"

"I mean . . . I guess that's true. But I always considered myself to be so transparent, so clumsy, that I guess I just figured she knew how hard it was for me to get where I am today."

"You know, this might sound obvious, but one of the downsides to making it look easy is that no one ever knows how hard it was."

"Ha. Yeah. Wow. I always wanted it to look easy. But maybe an unintended side effect was that when things got hard for Vera, she figured she was doing something wrong, because it all seemed so easy for me. I . . . never thought about it that way."

"Would you ever tell her about Vegas?"

"Oh, God. Maybe. I don't know. The idea of doing that is nails on a chalkboard. But . . . it bugs me though. I don't think she really gets how kickass she is. It's like she's always waiting for somebody to tell her why her idea is stupid and will never work. I just want her to see herself the way I see her."

". . ."

"JD? You still there?"

"Yeah. I know you guys have got your stuff, but you sound like a really good brother, Eliot."

"You said you have a brother, right?"

"Yeah."

"What's your relationship like?"

"Well, a few days ago I literally peeled him off a floor and then had to enlist my ex-boyfriend's help to drag him from the car into his house."

"Ouch. Shit. That's awful, JD. I'm so sorry to hear that."

"I wish I could say it was an anomaly."

"Is he an alcoholic?"

"I mean, he's never been diagnosed or anything like that, but he definitely doesn't have a good relationship with drinking. He's been to AA a few times, here and there. But it never stuck. The bingeing thing is mostly just on the weekends. He holds down his job well enough."

"What's his job?"

"He works for an electric company."

"That's good work."

"Really good. Union job. And thank God for that. He needs job security."

"Sounds like you take care of him in a lot of ways?"

"Oh. Yes and no. In case you can't tell, I'm not exactly the most nurturing person on the planet."

"What do you mean?"

"Oh, come on. I think my personality is pretty clear."

"Flaccid webcomic praise aside, I think you're actually really nurturing! You make me feel better all the time! You might not be the most . . . cuddly person I've ever met, but this way, when you're supportive, it actually means something. I know it's because I deserve it. Not just because that's who you are anyway. It's nice."

"Ironically, I'm probably one of the cuddliest people in real life you'll ever meet. Maybe not with my words. But physically."

"Really?"

"Yeah. I don't look like I would be, but I am. I'm a blanket hog, too."

"Interesting . . . So, you're a physically intimidating person who knows of my sister but isn't close friends with her. You've just helped me to cross about fifty prospective JDs off my list."

"Oh."

"Are you Rachel Ziegler?"

"Minus ten."

"Maxi Winters?"

"Minus ten."

"Sarah McCoy?"

"Minus ten."

"Oy. That was a bloodbath. What's my point count at now?"

"I don't know. Approximately negative a million?"

"Brutal. Okay, I finished the drawing. Let me just snap a pic and . . ."

"Wow. That's how you picture me, huh?"

"She-blob."

"This is actually significantly more flattering than I thought it would be."

"Really?"

"Yeah, there're boobs."

"That's how you know it's a *she*-blob."

"Right. Of course. I should have realized."

"I gave you a cool car, too. A Camaro. You can't tell because it's pencil but it's candy apple red in my head."

"Badass. You know, this is technically my first-ever portrait."

"I'll send you the original! You can frame it and put it up on the wall!"

"You angling for my address?"

"Huh? Oh. Right. Never mind. You know, if you told me who you are, we could just be friends already and it wouldn't be weird for me to mail you this picture."

"I'm pretty sure it would always be weird for you to mail me a portrait you drew of me as a blob driving a Camaro into the sky."

"Touché."

"I'm actually starting to get a little sleepy without the baking show. It's a miracle."

"Wait! I forgot I was supposed to be getting ready for bed. I'm way behind. I haven't even brushed my teeth yet. Wait!"

"Don't panic, I'm not going anywhere."

"I was hoping you'd say that. Did you brush your teeth yet? I didn't hear you."

"I did before we got on the line."

"And pajamas?"

"Are you really asking me what I'm wearing right now?"

"I mean . . . yes. But, like, in a non-creepy way?"

"Is there a non-creepy way to ask someone what they're wearing over the phone?"

"Hmmm. Let me try. How about: 'Hey, girl, tell me about your flannel PJ pants.' "

"That is officially the worst thing I've ever heard in my life. Booooooo."

"Okay, then, you try!"

"I don't have to try. I can already guess what you wear for pajamas."

"What? How?"

"Your personality makes it super obvious. You clearly wear matching plaid pajama sets with one of those button-up shirts with the floppy collar. You know, Christmas morning pajamas. Oh! And a long skinny cap with a ball on the end. With your slippers lined up perfectly beside the bed. And a glass of warm milk on the bedside table."

"Wow. So, basically you think of me as a total square."

"You're a good little boy, Eliot. Face it."

"No! I refuse! You're calling me a loser in so many words. I'm not a good little boy! I'm an M-A-N. My pajamas are, you know, made of steel wool. I eat chicken off the bone and throw the bones into the roaring campfire I stoke throughout the night. I sleep with a machete under my pillow."

"Of course. How could I have ever confused you for a sweet little softboy cinnamon roll? I'm sorry, that's my mistake."

"If you keep making that face, someday it's going to stick that way."

"How do you know what face I'm making?"

"How do you know what pajamas I'm wearing? Let's face it, JD—we know each other at this point."

"Hold on. Hold the phone. Stop everything. Back up. I . . . was right? You're actually wearing matching plaid pajamas with slippers and a cap?"

"No to the cap because I'm not living in a Charles Dickens novel. But I *might* be wearing plaid pajama pants that have a matching shirt somewhere in my closet, and I *might* have lined up some slippers beside the bed."

"Oh. My. God."

"Who doesn't have slippers?"

"*I* don't wear slippers."

"You just let your feet touch the cold floor in the morning like an animal?"

"I guess I'm not as civilized as you are, Hoffman."

"Someday, when this anonymity thing is far behind us and we really know each other, I'm going to mail you that portrait and a pair of slippers. They're gonna blow your mind. Once you go slippers, you never go back. You'll never be the same. They'll change you for life."

"See, this is why the anonymity thing is *important*. A strange man just told me he's going to mail me a pair of slippers and a picture of me that he drew. If that's not the beginning to a movie about a serial killer I don't know what is."

"Crap! You're right. Dang. Don't you ever wish that you could just, like, unzip your head and show somebody everything that's in there?"

"What do you mean?"

"Well, I'm not dangerous. I'm nice. I'm like the least threatening guy on the planet. I wear matching pajamas, for Christ's sake. I wish you could get an x-ray view of my thoughts and then you could see that you have absolutely nothing to fear from me."

"You know I'm not scared of you, Eliot. We've been through this. I know you well enough to know that you're not dangerous. And besides. I've seen you in person. I could definitely beat you in hand-to-hand combat."

"Is that an insult to me or a compliment to yourself?"

"Compliment to myself."

"Are you an athlete? A fighter or boxer or something?"

"I know my way around a gym."

"See, I should be taking notes right now. Instead of just saying 'yes,' you say, 'I know my way around a gym.' It's, like, so much cooler."

"Well, I *do* know my way around a gym."

"Do you lift or do classes or what?"

"I lift. Jump rope. Box a little. Sometimes I run."

"That is so badass. I didn't even know there were still gyms that offered that kind of stuff. I just got a fancy new gym membership and I'm thinking it was a total waste of money."

"Why?"

"Well, in the past, whenever I wanted to work out, I would just go for a run or play pickup basketball, or maybe join a soccer league if I was really feeling frisky."

"Uh-huh."

"I've never done the whole . . . designer gym thing before."

"Let me guess, is everybody really hot at your gym?"

"Oh, my God. It's ridiculous. I swear people are oiling themselves up before they work out. Everyone has perfect hair. And everyone already looks like they've been coming to the gym for years. There are literally zero beginners like me. So, the one and only time I went since I signed up, I just stood there in my stupid T-shirt with my, you know, *normal* body, and I just felt like such a loser. I don't even know how to use the machines."

"Can you hire a trainer for a session or two? They'll teach you how to use everything."

"I think I just signed up at the wrong place. It's not my scene. I just want to go somewhere that I can get a little stronger without being judged for my general incompetence. I need a confidence boost."

"Ugh. Dammit."

"What?"

"UGH!"

"JD? Everything all right?"

"Yes, everything is fine. I'm just about to do something really stupid because I like you and I want you to be happy."

"I . . . okay?"

"First of all, did you sign a contract at the designer gym?"

"Just a one-month."

"Great. Next month, when your contract is up, don't renew. Instead, go to this place called Geddy's. It's a little hole-in-the-wall boxer's gym."

"Oh! I've seen that place. The whole front of the gym is just a garage door?"

"Yeah. You have to drag it up and down to get inside. It makes it cold as hell during the winter, but the guy who runs it puts on space heaters. It's nothing fancy. *Seriously* nothing fancy. But they treat everybody with respect and they really don't care about aesthetics there. It's all about getting stronger within your own limits."

"Wow! That's so perfect! I . . . Thanks, JD."

"You're welcome."

"Why do you sound so disgruntled?"

"Because I'm ceding my territory to you."

"Ah. Well . . . how about this. If I sign up there, I'll let you know before I go. That way I won't ambush you or accidentally run into you. Cool?"

"Oh. Yeah. Actually that works."

"All right. So. Baking show and hopefully sweet, sweet oblivion?"

"You're all scrubbed up and ready for bed?"

"I even washed behind my ears."

"You really do live in a Dickens novel."

"I'm old-school like that."

"I think that's just called old."

"Well, considering I'm preparing myself to fall asleep in front of my favorite television program, I guess I won't argue with that."

"All we need are the reclining chairs and old, musty afghans over our legs."

"And the beer bellies."

"And the TV trays."

"Hey, JD?"

"Yeah?"

"Do you ever think about what a miracle it is that we started talking to one another? I mean, it's such a huge coincidence that the random letters I assigned to your contact happened to be next to my sister's in my phone. And that I never got around to changing it to your real name. And that when I messaged, you had nothing else to do but answer me. And that we both don't sleep well. And we both like reality television. And we're both willing to talk to one another for hours until we fall asleep almost every night. Do you ever think about that? What a miracle it is?"

"Eliot?"

"Yeah?"

"I think about it all the time."

Chapter Fifteen

Eliot

The next morning I swing by my local police precinct. Unfortunately, over the last two months, this has become a habit for me. Gloria, the receptionist, knows me by name now. I step into the main lobby and her face falls when she sees me, and correspondingly so does my stomach. Because that means that they've made no progress on my case. If they'd made progress, she would have lit up. She buzzes back for the detective assigned to my case and a few minutes later, Detective Cabela emerges from the back hallway, her hands tucked into her trousers and her badge on a chain around her neck.

She has a glum expression on her face and just a touch of a flush in her brown skin. Her dark hair is braided back today and she looks pretty. If she didn't sort of represent one of the worst nights of my life, I might have asked her out when we first met.

"Hi there, Mr. Hoffman."

"Detective."

She knows exactly why I'm there and she doesn't waste either of our time. That's one of the reasons I like her. She's got a real down-to-business vibe. "I'm sorry to tell you that we haven't made any progress on your case."

I sigh and look down. It's not a surprise to me. My case was nonviolent, had only my eyewitness account, and very few other leads. It's small potatoes and pretty much only important to me. But as someone who hasn't gotten a good night's sleep since it happened, I've been kind of clinging to the hope that apprehending the guy who did it might provide me with a little peace of mind.

"I figured," I tell her. "Just thought I'd check in."

"You know," she says with a cock of her head, "you could always just call me to check in on the status of the investigation."

"I know. I was just passing by anyhow."

Her eyes are kind with understanding. "And you don't want me forgetting about you."

"I know my case is low on the totem pole. I just want to stay on your radar."

"Mr. Hoffman," she says, and I can't help but notice the little bit of gravel in her voice. "I'm not going to forget about you. We're working your case as hard as we work any other."

A colleague of hers calls her name and she waves at me as she gets back to work. I leave the precinct with my hands in my pockets and my eyes on the sidewalk. I halt halfway down the block and look back at the police station.

I've kind of been thinking that if and when I happen to see JD in person, after all that time talking to one another, I would just kind of *know* it was her. Not anything as cheesy as a bolt of lightning. But maybe like a low-level surge of awareness. I'll see JD and everything will just make sense. Right?

I pull my phone out and search for Detective Cabela in my contacts. There's nothing there. Did she mean that I could call the precinct to contact her? Or was she implying that at some point we exchanged numbers? Is it possible that she's a mislabeled contact in my address book?

I start walking again, cursing myself for not asking Detective Cabela to call me by my first name. I'm positive that if I heard her say *Eliot*, I would know whether or not she's JD. Or, hell, I could have just asked her straight out.

"Hey . . . any chance that you're JD?" I practice, asking the air in front of me with a casual flip of my hand, as if it doesn't matter to me either way.

"No. But any chance you're a crazy person?" my sister asks from beside me, appearing out of thin air and basically scaring me into the next dimension.

"OH MY GOD."

"Hahahhahahaha. Wow. You should see yourself right now." Judging from her reaction she's never seen anything funnier than this.

"I imagine my hair is sticking straight up?"

"That jump-scare pretty much blew the eyebrows off your face just now."

"Were you walking home from the train?"

"Yup."

It's then I realize that she's shlepping an armful of shipping materials and that I should probably give my baby sister a hand.

"Thanks," she says, quickly handing off 90 percent of the stuff in her arms. "Why were you talking to yourself?"

"Oh, I was just practicing something."

"Practicing asking someone who they are?"

I feel a flush rising from under my collar. I tell Vera about almost everything in my life, but over the last two months, I've been keeping a fair amount from her. Should I just tell her about JD? Eh, I don't exactly feel like getting teased about it at this particular moment. "Something like that."

I'm four steps past her before I realize she's stopped walking. "Wait. Eliot . . . are you dating?"

"What? What makes you say that?"

"Well, you were practicing asking someone if they were who you thought they were. And the only times I've ever done that have been when I've met up with Tinder dates."

"Ah." Because it's not exactly a lie, I go along with her story. "Yeah. I've been sort of starting something up with someone? I think? But we're still just at the phone stage and anyway it's probably nothing. To answer your question—yes. I'm a crazy person."

My house is closer than Vera's and I want to get her off this topic so I jump in with a suggestion. "Wanna come over for dinner?"

"Oh. Sure!"

She's never passed up a home-cooked meal in her life. But as we walk up to my apartment building I see a scrum of my neighbors all standing out on the front sidewalk and a firetruck parked in the middle of the street. It's got lights on but no sirens.

"What's going on?" I ask John Matley, a neighbor who lives two floors up from me.

"Oh, nothing. The building-wide fire alarm got tripped, but there's no fire or anything. They're just doing a quick check of the building before they let us all back in."

"Let's just drop this stuff off at your place," I suggest to Vera. "We can either order takeout there or come back to mine afterward."

We get to Vera's and order burritos, but when I walk back over to my house a couple hours later, the alarm is still going off inside my building. The fire truck is gone, but the neighbors are still mostly outside. Half of them look exhilarated and the other half look exasperated. I can see our super pacing halfway down the block on the phone with someone. And man, she looks pissed. I'm more than relieved to not be whoever is on the receiving end of that phone call.

Frida, my downstairs neighbor, sees me and makes a beeline. If there's news, she's going to want to be the one to deliver it. In fact, I'm sure she was devastated to find out that John Matley had filled me in on the rest.

"Electrical issue with the alarm, apparently." She doesn't even bother with a casual hello. Her eyes are alight with excitement. This is easily the most thrilling thing that has happened to her in months, I can already tell.

"The new super's on the line with the alarm company but they're telling her that it's an electrical issue so apparently she's also got the old super on the line with the electrical company. But they don't think they'll make it for a few hours at least."

"Are we allowed to go in?"

"Sure, if you can stand the noise."

I quickly call Vera and confirm that I can spend the night on her couch before I jog into the building and plug my ears as I head up the stairs to my apartment. This alarm is no joke and it almost brings tears to my eyes when I have to drop one hand to unlock my apartment door. There is definitely something screwy with the electricity right now because my security system has been knocked out and the lights I normally leave on in the apartment are off.

I take one step inside and freeze. It's the first time since I had it installed two months ago that I'll be entering my apartment without having to disable the alarm first. Which means it's the first time in two months that I'm not completely certain there's no one else in here with me.

A chill tightens the skin all over my body, and I bounce on my toes, hesitating on the threshold.

"This is my apartment," I tell myself, trying to ignore the

eerie way the bright, strobing light from the fire alarm is making everything alternate between a ghostly white and then shadowy black. "This is my house."

I have to go in and get some stuff. So I take a deep breath and jet straight toward my bathroom. The first thing I do is scramble through my medicine cabinet for some earplugs. Once they're in place I feel better. Now I have two hands at the ready for whatever might come and the earsplitting shriek of the alarm has been dulled down to a manageable degree.

I'm sweating and not because of exertion. My hands are shaking as I drag an overnight bag out of my closet.

"There's no one else here," I reassure myself, and turn around all at once, knowing that if I turn in degrees, I'll freak myself out even more. The only thing I see is my empty apartment, bathed in light and then bathed in shadow.

I head to the bedroom and grab clothes at random. Next is my toothbrush and last is all the equipment I need for work. I'm breathing a huge sigh of relief as I lock my apartment door behind me.

The worst part of what happened two months ago is that it turned my apartment into enemy territory. I shouldn't be more relieved to be in the stairwell than I was to be in my own home. But here we are.

I take the stairs two at a time and I'm huffing for oxygen by the time I skid back out onto the street.

The group of neighbors out front all look up at me in a mixture of surprise and confusion. Probably because I've got my hands on my knees while I gasp for air and there's a half-zipped backpack slipping off one shoulder.

Suddenly there's a firm hand on my elbow and I quickly straighten. I'm standing ten inches away from my super, looking down into her concerned face. From this distance I notice that in addition to the septum piercing she actually has a small eyebrow piercing I've never noticed before. I probably notice now because her eyebrows are pulled forward into a tight knot. She's lined with concern for me.

I see her lips form the words, "Are you all right?" but there's no sound that accompanies it.

"Oh. Earplugs," I say, surely way too loud. I go to remove them but before I can answer her question her phone lights up in her hand and she turns away to answer it.

I put the earplugs in my pocket and wave to my neighbors as I start the walk to Vera's. It's almost ten o'clock, but the walk is brightly lit and almost cheery. It's a warm enough night that every few houses there are people sitting on their stoops, smoking or talking or just watching the night pass by.

I've always loved this city. I've been living here since I was eighteen years old. Which means I've lived here almost as long as I lived in my hometown. April and May are by far my two favorite months. When people are just starting to poke their heads out of the ground. When they're happy to be out in the world, but still sleepy after a long winter. When everyone is just relieved that, yup, in fact the seasons do still change after all. In my mind, it's the most relaxed time of year. Everyone is looking forward to the summer, but no one is grumpy about the hot weather yet.

This is the time of year when the streets in my neighborhood almost feel like an extension of my home. I usually feel comfortable. But right now I can't ignore the clammy sweat at my back. I think messaging with JD has been so fun this week that I was starting to think things were turning around for me. But now, I realize that this has all just been a distraction. I'm not moving on. I'm just pretending it didn't happen.

I'm standing on the sidewalk in front of Vera's apartment

building, but before I buzz up to her apartment I have one more thing I have to do.

I pull out my phone and call JD.

It rings five and a half times before she answers.

"Eliot?"

"Hey. I didn't think you were gonna answer."

"Yeah. Sorry."

"Are you jogging?"

"Huh?"

"You sound super out of breath."

"Oh. Yeah. I'm jogging."

"At ten p.m.?"

"Uh-huh."

"Okay. Well, I'll let you get back to it. I was just calling to say that I'm staying at my sister's house tonight because of some stuff going on at my apartment, so I probably wasn't going to be able to talk anyhow."

"Oh . . . Is everything okay?"

"Yeah. It's just an electrical issue with the fire alarm. No big deal."

"Eliot?"

"Yeah?"

"You sound a little . . . off."

"Are you this perceptive all the time? Or have we just gotten to know each other pretty well?"

"Both? Maybe?"

"JD, I wish . . ."

"Yeah?"

"I wish that I could drop my stuff off at my sister's and then invite you out for a beer."

"That . . . sounds nice."

"I wanna sit on a barstool and look up and see you walking

through the door and feel that . . . thing people feel when they're sitting in a room full of strangers and then someone they know walks in. You know that feeling, JD? It's somewhere between relief and . . . and . . . joy? I don't know. It's like when you're in a room full of people you don't know, somewhere in the back of your head it starts to feel like maybe that room is the whole world, but then the person you're waiting for comes in and you remember that you're not alone in the world? That you have *that* person right there. And that they came all the way there to sit next to you? Do you know that feeling?"

"Yeah. I know that feeling."

"Well, I want that to happen. I want to cheers with you and . . . and . . . know who I'm talking to. *I wanna know who I'm talking to, JD*. Is that too much to ask? You know me well enough to hear in my voice that something isn't right but *I don't even know your name*."

"Eliot—"

"Look. I'm sorry. Don't mind me. I'm low-key freaking out and it has nothing to do with you or this conversation. I'm sorry. I'm making this about one thing when it's probably about something else. Just forget what I said. I'm sorry. I think I'm triggered or something. I feel dizzy."

"Eliot, where are you right now?"

"I'm out front of my sister's place."

"Does she know you're there?"

"She's expecting me."

"All right. Listen to me. In a second, we're gonna hang up, and you're gonna go up to your sister's apartment. You're gonna tell her you're really tired, and then you're gonna curl up, tuck yourself in, and watch a Disney movie. Okay? No cutting corners. I mean an *actual* Disney movie. Pick one. And tomorrow, we can talk about all of this. I promise we'll talk about all of it, okay?"

"... Okay."

"And send me a selfie once you're inside so I know you didn't get abducted by aliens between the time we hang up and you walk inside, okay?"

"I can't believe you're angling for a selfie at a time like this."

"Eliot!"

"Just teasing you. Okay. You're right. I'll go inside and take care of myself. You finish your jog. I'll send you the pic."

"Sleep well, Eliot."

"Sleep well, JD."

Chapter Sixteen

Jessie

The next morning I find myself looking at Eliot's selfie for probably the nine hundredth time. It's blurry and unflattering and the lighting is terrible. He's on his back, tucked into what looks like a couch, giving me a crooked thumbs-up. I couldn't love it more.

The tone of his voice last night sits in my memory like a cactus, pricking me from every side. He was so upset. And he wanted comfort. From his friend. Who he's obviously come to care about.

He wants more. With me.

And I can't give it. I can never be the person who walks into the bar and gives him that feeling. I can't even tell him that he doesn't have to explain why he was triggered last night.

It's been a hell of a few days at work so I ask Pops's friend Carl if he could be on call for me. He agrees immediately and I'm relieved. If anybody needs anything for the next couple of hours, I'll just pass the message on to Carl. With that said and done I grab my helmet and get on my bike. It's just a touch too warm for my leather jacket and pants, but when I built the motorcycle, Pops made me promise that I'd never ride it without leather. In case of an accident, leather is the safest protection that anyone could be wearing, and it was an easy promise to make. Once I start riding, the breeze cools me down anyhow.

I have to fight traffic until I get out toward the ocean, but then it's smooth sailing. I cruise the last stretch of Flatbush until it turns into the Marine Parkway Bridge and then I'm hit full in the face with fresh, salty air. The sun is diamond-bright against the water and I'm glad I wore my helmet with the sun-visor.

Far Rockaway is by far my favorite part of New York City. Especially at this time of year, when the sun is warm but the summer crowds haven't descended yet. I wind through Fort Tilden and park my bike in a shady little lot next to a sandy road that leads to the beach. There's golden grass as tall as I am on one side of me, and if it weren't for the almost-constant low-flying planes on their way to or from JFK, you could almost forget you were within the city limits.

I make it out to the beach and, as expected, the water is rough with whitecaps. Like most things in New York City, the beaches on Far Rockaway are not for the weak. This is the kind of beach that knocks you on your ass and gets sand up your bathing suit. In fact, one of my earliest memories is getting knocked over by an unexpected wave, salt water up my nose and sand burn on my cheek. And then there was Pops, lifting me out of the ocean with one big hand, throwing me on his back and making me howl with laughter as he showed me how hard it is to run forward when the waves are heading back out to sea.

It's in that moment, with the April sun bright on the top of my head and the shiny silver ocean tossing itself against the sand, that I'm absolutely socked in the face with emotion. My vision blurs with tears and I gasp for breath as I crouch down. I don't know how else to explain it. I miss my dad. Which is ridiculous, because I saw him two days ago and I talked to him on the phone just this morning. But it is what it is.

He's dying. It's slow and terrible, and there's absolutely nothing I can do about it but help him get his affairs in order.

I've tried so hard not to bother him with all of my problems because in the face of his diagnosis, everything else just seemed so trivial. But the thing is, that means I just haven't been dealing with anything that's happened to me this year. I haven't been turning to Pops. So I haven't been turning to anybody.

I'm sitting in the sand and crying like a nine-year-old so I decide to fully engage with that feeling. I need my dad right now.

I pull my phone out of my pocket and call him.

"Hey, kid," he answers.

"Dad."

"What happened?"

"How do you know something's wrong?" I demand.

"You only ever call me 'Dad' when you're really upset. Where are you? It sounds windy." His voice is slightly gravelly, like he's been sleeping, and I wonder guiltily if I woke him. He needs all the sleep he can get right now.

"I'm at Fort Tilden."

"You're not staring out at the ocean and contemplating my mortality, are you? That would be super lame, kid."

"I miss you."

"Miss me? We talked this morning."

"No, I mean I miss you . . . preemptively." I wince at how that ends up sounding.

"Kid . . ."

"I know. It's stupid. I know it's stupid. You're right there and

I can drive up and see you whenever I want, but . . . everything is just so . . ."

"It's so what?"

"So different than how it used to be."

"Look. I know it wasn't an easy decision for you to take over my job—" I hear the worry and regret laced into his tone and I want to squash it from existence.

"No! No, that's not it. I'm actually starting to like it. It's good work. And you took such good care of everything for so long that there's barely any work for me to do."

"You've always been a shitty liar."

"Well, it's a hard job. You know that better than anyone."

"So, it's not the work. What is it? . . . Your brother?" he guesses.

". . ."

"Kid, if there's something wrong with Jack, you gotta tell me."

"He's fine. He's safe. He just did some more dumb shit and now . . ."

"Now you've gotta clean it up?"

"Something like that. Honestly, Pops, the less you know about this one the better."

". . ."

"Pops?"

"That's not it," he says after a moment.

"Huh?"

"I can hear it in your voice. There's something more. It's not just about Jack. What is it?"

"Sometimes it's a pain in the ass to be so easy to read. I end up having to tell you everything."

"Isn't that why you called me? To tell me everything?"

"Good point."

"So. Tell me."

". . . I think I'm falling in love?" Even though he can't see me, I cover my face with one hand.

"Oh, boy."

"What's with that tone?"

"I plead the fifth."

"Pops, don't be a dick."

"What, you want me to click my heels for you?"

"Well, you don't have to be a total downer about it."

"The words 'I'm in love' haven't exactly ever been good news for our family, kid," he says.

"What's that supposed to mean?"

"The last person Jack loved was that Melody person who stole his car. The last person you loved was Trent, who, God love him, is a total asshole. And the last person I loved was your mother and I don't even need to explain—"

"Can we not? Can we just not talk about her? Or compare what I'm feeling to what you and her had together? Okay? This is completely different than that. And it's not like I'm a total goner for this guy or anything. I'm at, like, the very, very *beginning* of falling in love. With someone who is totally different than anyone I've ever been into before. Like, pretty much the opposite."

"The opposite of someone you've been with before . . . so, he's not a meathead. He's a good listener. And he's a dork?"

"Thanks for that, Pops. I'm pretty sure you're roasting me right now, aren't you?"

"Am I wrong?" he asks in that know-it-all tone of his that I've always pretended to hate but secretly love.

"No. Except for the dork part. I mean he is *kind of* a dork, but in a good way. A cute way."

"So, what's the problem, then?"

"Jack."

". . . Jack doesn't like him or something?" he asks.

"No. It's not that. Jack doesn't even know him. But Eliot knows Jack. And if he found out he was my brother he would . . . probably never want to speak to me again."

"I don't get it."

"I can't explain it more than that, Pops."

He pauses for a long moment, and I think he's going to demand more information, but instead, he surprises me. "Well, if it were me, and I was really in love with someone, I probably wouldn't give a damn who her dumbass brother is."

"I mean, it might not make him hate me. But he's definitely not going to want to come around for Christmas. It's a non-starter. There's no way we could have a real relationship if he couldn't be around Jack at all."

"So . . . this is about loyalty to Jack?"

"You sound surprised. He's my brother, Pops. I'm not going to cut him out of my life, no matter how much of a cut-up he's been."

"Have you talked to Jack about it?"

"No."

"Does he know you love this guy?"

"No," I say.

"Talk to him. He might surprise you. I don't know the situation, but there might be something he could do about it?"

"I'll think about it."

"Kid, there's something I've been thinking I should probably explain about your mom."

"Pops, I already know everything."

"What makes you so sure about that?"

"I was there, remember? It's not like you and Mom used to leave the room to fight with each other. I know why she left."

"..."

"Pops? You still there?"

"You take your bike out to the ocean?" Again, he surprises me by letting the topic drop.

"Huh? Oh. Yup."

"Ugh. I shouldn't have asked. Don't tell me any more. You're wearing your helmet? Your leather?"

"I thought I wasn't supposed to tell you any more."

"Kid . . ."

"Yes. Just like I promised."

"You're a good kid. You know that, right?" he asks. And there's something in his tone that tells me he's actually asking. He really wants to make sure I know.

"I'm painfully aware. I think my life would be a lot easier if I were rotten."

"You couldn't be rotten if you tried. Now, get off the beach before you catch cold. Go home. Do your job. Call your brother. Eat a good dinner. Go to bed at a reasonable hour. There. Did I do it right? Did I say everything a good dad is supposed to say?"

"Did you pull a muscle?"

"Shaddap," he says with a laugh.

"Love you, Pops."

"Love you, too, kid."

Instead of calling Jack or heading back to the house, I ride my bike straight to Geddy's gym. I park my bike and head in. It's afternoon so the gym is much more crowded than I usually see it when I come in the early morning. Raoul's eyes widen when he sees me.

"Not your usual workout time," he says, crossing his arms over his chest and cocking his head.

"I'm not here to work out. I actually had a question for you."

He waves me over to the side of the gym so that we're well

away from the two teenagers messily sparring with one another. Raoul's got one eye on them and one on me. His expression tightens and he takes a step toward the kids when one of them yelps, but another one of his trainers catches the mistake and steps in. Raoul relaxes and leans against the wall, focusing on me.

"Shoot."

"Well, I was wondering if you've ever dealt with clients who've gone through . . . traumatic stuff before."

"What do you mean?"

"Well, there's someone I know who I want to come work out here. But he's not really a fighter, you know? I think he's been going through a hard time. I thought getting stronger, maybe some self-defense kind of stuff, would help ease his mind a little bit. I recommended he come here, but then I was wondering if a boxing gym was the best place for somebody who . . . doesn't like to fight."

"Ah. Yeah. I get it. Sure. A lot of guys come here just for the exercise. The camaraderie. But it's good for the soul, too. Boxing. It's helped a lot of my guys get through hard times."

"You've dealt with that before? Trauma?"

"Sure. Not everybody likes to hit or get hit. Some people like it too much. I've been doing this a long time. I can usually tell what somebody needs or doesn't need."

"All right. That's good to know. I think he'll come by in the next month or so. He wants to quit his other gym."

"Why don't you bring him around next time you come? Introduce me."

I shift uncomfortably. I haven't had to say this part out loud to anyone yet and I highly doubt Raoul will understand. Anonymous chatting might be a bit of a question mark for him.

"Um. Well. I don't actually know him."

He raises one eyebrow that does all the talking for him.

"Well, to be exact," I stutter, wondering if I'm in the process of losing all my cred with Raoul, "he doesn't know who *I* am. And I'd like to keep it that way."

"Keep what *what* way?"

"Ah. Look. It's complicated but he's a good guy. Eliot Hoffman. Treat him well when he comes in. But just don't mention me. At all. Even if he asks. Which he probably won't. He's respectful of our . . . situation. But just don't tell him anything about me. I just wanted to check and make sure that this was gonna be a good fit for him, since I told him to come. But it looks like it's gonna work out. So just, yeah. Train him or whatever, but keep me out of it."

Throughout the course of my speech, Raoul's face gets tighter and tighter and by the end, I can barely see his lips anymore, they're pressed so tight together.

"Girl, I do not understand this situation."

"He and I are anonymously chatting, okay? And I really like him, but I'm not ready for him to find out my identity."

"Oh, lord." Raoul covers his face with one leathery paw. "Don't tell me this is some internet sex thing, is it? Not you. Not Lou's girl. What am I going to tell Lou?"

I'm sure my face is tomato-red right now. This is not a conversation I ever wanted to have with Raoul. But *especially* not in person. "Oh, my God! No! It's not that, and my dad already knows about this whole thing, okay? Just—"

"Dad, don't jump to conclusions."

I startle a little, because I didn't realize that Ronnie was standing right behind me. Which means that he's heard this conversation as well. Lovely.

Ronnie is sweaty from a workout and looking highly embarrassed, but not judgmental. He glances down at me. "He always jumps to the worst conclusions. Too much *Dateline*."

I laugh, a little surprised. It's the closest thing to a joke Ronnie has ever said in front of me.

"Send your guy our way," Ronnie continues. "We'll take care of him."

"Oh. Thanks."

Raoul gives me one last suspicious look before the sparring kids catch his attention again and he jogs off to reprimand them. I'm left standing beside a sweaty Ronnie, embarrassed, grateful, and awkward.

"Is it, like, an online dating thing?" Ronnie asks after a second, brushing imaginary dust off his shorts.

"Oh. No. Actually it's more of a wrong-number situation. We got to talking and kind of hit it off."

"You're kidding." His eyes sparkle, and I suddenly realize that I've never really looked Ronnie full in the face before. He's got tawny skin like his dad, and lots of black curly hair tied into a knot on the top of his head. He's nice-looking when he's not staring at the floor. "That's so . . . cute."

"Oh. Yeah. I guess it's cute. For now or whatever. We don't really have a future or anything. I'm not gonna tell him who I really am."

"Oh." Ronnie looks disappointed. "Well, you never know, I guess."

Silence descends, and I try to figure out a way to non-awkwardly extricate myself from this conversation and this gym.

"I'm glad . . . either way, though," Ronnie says after a minute. "That you brought that up to my dad."

"Oh. Why?"

"Well, now he'll think you're involved with someone and he'll stop trying to get me to propose marriage to you with every spare minute he has."

"Oh, God." I immediately cover the bottom half of my face with one hand. I don't want him to see the half bemused, half mortified expression I'm sure I'm wearing.

"I can see from your reaction that he's been pushing this on you, too?"

I let the hand drop and glance up at Ronnie. "Well, he's not exactly subtle."

"I'm sorry if it made you uncomfortable. I kept telling him, *Dad, she's the only female member you have, you can't keep trying to set us up.*"

"I'm just glad that it's . . ."

"Over?" he supplies with a little half-smile on his face. "Don't worry. I just started dating somebody, too. It's, um, really new. And I really wasn't sure it was going to work out. But yeah." He gets a sheepish look on his face. "It's, uh, working out. Once I bring them home to meet him, I'm pretty sure Dad won't bother you again."

"Oh. Well, congrats on that." I give him an awkward wave. "I'm gonna head out."

"Just one more thing."

I turn back to look at him. "Yeah?"

"My dad is too nosy. Too pushy. But he's also a really excellent judge of character. And if even half of what he's told me about you is true, then you sound like a really amazing person. Really loyal. Plus you're cute. I just . . . this is out of line, but I just made things work with my person and I'm all hopped up on pheromones and whatever and I know it's not my business but I just wanted to say that I hope that if you've really decided not to meet this guy . . . I just hope you're seeing yourself clearly, is all."

"Oh. Thanks, Ronnie. I'll keep that in mind." I start to walk away and then stop and turn back to him one more time. I gesture at my motorcycle jacket and leather pants. "Cute?"

He shrugs. "Badass?"

"Much better."

He smiles. I smile. I walk out of the gym feeling significantly better than I did when I woke up this morning.

And I know exactly the reason.

Because I got to *do* something for Eliot. Maybe it wasn't a lot, talking to Raoul, making sure the gym was the right place for Eliot. But still. It was something. Someone I care about is hurting and I was able to do something that would hopefully help.

See, that's the thing about this whole anonymous, ultimately doomed relationship. You'd think that the tough part would be never getting to go out on a date with Eliot. Or kiss him goodnight. Or wake up next to him. All the fun stuff. But the even worse part is that it robs me, him, us, of the hard stuff, too.

If I never tell him who I am, I'm never going to take care of him when he's sick. I'm never going to drive across the city to pick him up if his car breaks down. I'm never going to console him if he loses a job. I'm never going to get up early to take his trash out because he forgot to do it the night before.

I park the bike outside of my building, but I don't get off. For a long breath, I just sit there. My gut is filled with clown balloons. Because I've just realized how good it feels to do something for Eliot.

When Ronnie was describing me, he said "loyal," and he wasn't wrong. Because maybe, just maybe, in this particular situation, my brother isn't the only one who deserves my loyalty.

Is it possible to do right by one of them without betraying the other? I've been thinking of Eliot and Jack as standing on opposite sides of the road, with me in the middle. To walk toward one of them is to turn my back on the other one. But maybe there's a way? Maybe there's a way with both of them by my side?

I take off my helmet and tuck it under my arm. I call my brother. I'm striding away from the building because I don't want anyone I know to overhear this conversation. An absurd amount of disappointment swamps me when I get his voicemail. I really thought that maybe if he answered, I'd magically be able to say something to him like I'd just said to Raoul. *There's this man named Eliot*, I'd tell him. *He's gotten banged up, but help me treat him right. Help me fix this, Jack.*

The thought of saying those words aloud to Jack turns my blood into water, puts sweat down my back. But it's the only way out of this, isn't it? The only way I can ever hear Eliot say my name, my real name, and know who I am, is if I'm locked and loaded with Jack's blessing.

I try Jack one more time, but he doesn't answer then either. I send him a quick text telling him to call me when he gets a chance, but there's a very high probability that a return call will never happen. If I really want to talk with him in the next few days, I might have to track him down.

I sigh and tuck my phone away.

Patience, I remind myself. Patience. But now that I see a potential solution, I want to sprint. Every moment I spend in limbo makes me feel like Eliot is slipping away.

The evening light is starting to change, but it's still warm, and I know that when I get back home, I'm going to take over for Carl and my quasi-day off will be completely over. I want to prolong this feeling for just a little bit longer. So, I turn away from my apartment building, deciding to take a stroll around the neighborhood, and—I'm sure this won't come as a surprise—I call Eliot.

Chapter Seventeen

"Hey, JD."

"Hey . . . what's wrong?"

"Oh. Nothing. I'm just kind of embarrassed about my freak-out last night."

"What? Why?"

"Okay, I think it's time I came clean about some stuff."

". . . Okay."

"You know how you wanted to make sure that I wasn't thinking of you as Zaza Habib?"

"Gigi Hadid, but sure."

"Right. Well, you know I'm not, like, The Rock. Right?"

". . . You mean Dwayne 'The Rock' Johnson?"

"Yeah."

"Yes, Eliot. I'm aware that you are not pro-wrestler-turned-actor Dwayne 'The Rock' Johnson. You forget that I've *met* you."

"I know. I know. But I just want to make sure that secretly, in your heart, you're not hoping I'm some sort of he-man."

"Not a he-man. Got it."

"Let's see . . . what else? Oh! I'm ridiculously annoying about recycling. And composting. Like, it irritates everyone. If I ever came over to your house, there's a good chance I'd sort your trash while you were in the bathroom."

"I recycle as well, so that wouldn't be a problem."

"Okay. I *can* drive a stick. Which is cool. But I *can't* change a tire. Which is not cool. I've tried. And failed."

"You should really learn! That's just negligent if you regularly drive a car."

"See? I'm sure you know how to change a tire. You can probably put together Ikea furniture without the instructions, can't you?"

"No one can do that. Eliot, what's going on right now? What's with this list you're giving me?"

"I'm making sure you know everything before I explain one more thing to you."

"You're making sure I know everything . . .?"

"Yeah. Okay. I thought of another one. And this one's a doozy. I do this one thing that would be really, really creepy if anyone ever found out about it in the wrong context."

"What is it? It's something gross, isn't it. I knew you were a closet perv."

"No! What? What do you mean *you knew* I was a closet perv?"

"It's always the nice ones."

"I'm . . . not even going to validate that with a response."

"Tell me what it is!"

"No way. You called me a perv so now I'm not going to tell you."

"Tell me or I take away fifty points."

"*Fifty?!* God, you don't play fair. Fine. I'll tell you . . . I draw people I know."

"Drawing people? That's the thing you think would be creepy if people found out? God, you really are a pure soul, Eliot. You need to get out more. Or stay in more. Have you ever even been on the internet before? There's a lot for you to learn."

"Let me explain how it could be considered weird."

"Okay."

"I draw people I know from memory."

"I'm failing to see how this is creepy. Are you saying you do it like over and over again and tack their faces up on your wall like a serial killer?"

"No. But I draw them doing . . . stuff."

"Sex stuff? You really are a perv, you perv!"

"No! Oh, my God. *You're* the perv, since yours is the mind that went there."

"Well, why did you pause so long before saying 'stuff'? What was I supposed to think?"

"I draw them doing things that are *comforting*. Everyday things. Things to humanize them. But it's never things I've actually seen them doing before, which is why it would be creepy if someone found the notebook."

"Examples, please."

"Okay. For instance, my old boss at work. He's—for lack of a better word—fratty. And he and I never saw eye to eye. But I realized that I was kind of stereotyping him in my head so I did a few portraits of him putting on eye makeup and lipstick in the mirror."

". . ."

"You still there?"

"Yes, just absorbing. So, you drew him putting on makeup and it made you get along with him better?"

"Yeah. I have no idea if he puts on makeup in his private life or not, but that's not the point. The point was reminding myself that I only see one small sliver of who this man is. His work self. And he has a million other facets that I'll likely never see. And by assuming I knew who he was . . . well, it was making me judge him and get frustrated with him. Drawing him like that was actually really cathartic. But if he'd ever found the portraits . . ."

"You'd have gotten fired."

"Most likely."

"That is freaking awesome. This is, like, the most healthy way of processing emotions I've ever heard. Give me more examples."

"Okay . . . when I was in the process of applying for a small business loan to get the design equipment I needed, I drew a series of pictures of the loan officer dog-paddling in a pool with, like, little swimmies on."

"Amazing. More."

"A couple days ago I just finished one of my super."

". . . Oh?"

"Yeah. She's the strong, silent type, and I'm always the biggest idiot whenever I'm around her. Like, honestly. She literally had to screw in a light bulb for me the other day."

"Uh-huh."

"She's got tats and piercings and stuff and a really . . . fierce face, so I did some portraits of her doing really . . . disarming stuff."

"What kind of disarming stuff?"

"In one she's trying to climb out of a ball pit."

"A ball pit?"

"Yeah, like at Chuck E. Cheese? No one can look cool while trying to extricate themselves from one of those."

"That is so freaking weird, Eliot."

"I told you I was weird!"

"Can you speak up a little? I'm trying to hear you over this siren. And I still don't understand why you're telling me all this stuff."

"Is that siren on your end or my end? And I guess I just want you to know about all the little weird or annoying things about me. Because I've tried to be interesting and fun on these phone calls, but I want you to have the whole picture. Because I'm about to tell you something that might make you think less of me. So I wanted to pad it with some other information about me that will make you see me as a regular guy. Not some inflated, imaginary version of myself."

"Okay. Check. I already don't do that anyhow. But now you've officially prepared me for the fact that you are a regular human man. Sorry I'm yelling! I can barely hear myself think!"

"Great. Now I want to explain why I was freaking out so much last night."

"Eliot. You don't actually have to explain."

"No, I want to."

"Okay, but just wait until the siren—*oof!* Oh, shit. Sorry! I . . ."

"Oh, my God."

Chapter Eighteen

Eliot

I stand back and blink down at the woman I just ran into. We both turned the corner too fast and *bam*, smashed right into each other. She's got her phone pressed to her ear and so do I. I've got one hand in the air in a natural, "hands away" sort of pose, but she's balancing herself against my chest. I realize now that I was hearing that police siren both through JD's end of the line and with my own ears.

Because that cop car was going by both of us. Because we are in exactly the same place. Because the person I'm staring at is JD. I can feel that my mouth is open but I can't make myself close it.

We stare at one another as the police car passes us. I can hear the siren next to me and through the phone. When the police car is gone we're both still just staring at one another. She's gone white as a sheet.

"JD." It's a statement. Not a question. Because I've never been more sure of anything in my life.

Suddenly, she animates. She hangs up our call, slips her phone in her pocket, and turns to walk the other way.

"Wait!" I call to her. "I—"

I would chase after her, but my feet are glued to the

sidewalk. Besides. Let's really think about what I'm dealing with right now. This is a woman who did not want me to know her identity. Probably, I'm realizing, because she lives in my building and I technically help pay her salary. And she just power-walked away from me on the street. If this were a television show, I'd probably be expected to run after her and make a speech. But this is real life. And in real life, you don't chase down women on the street when they've made it very clear that they want to put a lot of distance between the two of you.

But still.

I watch her long legs eat up the rest of the block and then she turns the corner into our apartment building.

I cannot believe it's her.

I cannot believe I know who JD is.

"Why were you staring in horror at our superintendent?" Frida Hawkins asks me as she appears at my elbow.

"Whoa!" I jump an inch off the ground. "How long have you been there?"

"Long enough to see you look at Jessie like you just realized she was Pennywise the Clown."

"Jessie." I hate so much that I'm learning JD's real name from Frida. I also hate that I was too much of a twerp to ask again for my new super's name after I forgot it the first time.

"Horror, you said?" I ask Frida in confusion. "That wasn't horror on my face. That was shock."

"Looked like horror to me."

Okay, so if I'm being honest with myself, there might have been a dash of horror mixed in to my expression.

How do I explain this?

All right, it's probably pertinent to explain about the first night I met JD. I mean Jessie. She was Jessie before she was JD. She's still Jessie. She was always Jessie.

God. Maybe if I hadn't met her on the worst night of my life I wouldn't have such a hard time merging JD and Jessie into one person. But here we are.

It was two and a half months ago. I used to sleep like the dead. Passed out in a pile. I used to need two different alarm clocks placed in different locations to get me out of bed. I used to sleep like a champ. But that night I blinked awake at 3 a.m. Something had pulled me out of my dream. I still remember that in the dream I was in a bookstore but every time I went to pull a book off the shelf it would end up being a sandwich.

Regardless, I sat up in bed and froze because I heard a noise coming from my living room. It was a crunching sort of thump. And then there were footsteps.

Someone was in my apartment.

My sister had a key, sure. But she'd never wear boots in the house and I was certain that this was the tread of a grown man.

So there I was, in boxer shorts, standing next to my bed, trying to decide what the hell to do next.

Here's the thing. Because of my tendency to get obsessed with things really easily, I always used to sleep with my phone in a different room. If I left it beside the bed, I might blink back into reality to realize that I'd been playing Bubble Shooter for the last four hours and now it was dawn. It was just generally healthier to charge it in the other room every night.

But at that particular moment, it meant that there was an intruder between me and my phone.

So, that's how I found myself in my underwear with a baseball bat in my hand. I keep one in all my closets just like my dad taught me. I played Little League and was actually pretty good as a kid. I probably could have made the high school team but at the time my grades weren't good enough. But right at that moment, I felt like I'd never touched a bat in my life. It was awkward and cold in my hands. I debated for a stupidly long amount of time whether or not I should take a second to put pants on. But then I imagined the intruder coming into my bedroom while I had my pants halfway up and me having to fight for my life while tripping around like an idiot.

Underwear was best, I figured. So, there I went, sneaking down the hallway toward the living room. Bat in hand.

I crept around the corner and saw the mess before I saw the man.

I'd apparently slept through a lot because all the books were off the shelves. I could see that the vase where I'd hidden a couple hundred bucks in emergency cash was tipped to one side and empty. My couch was disheveled, the blankets on the floor.

Carefully, quietly, I stepped around the corner into the living room. My eyes were focused on the window across the room, the desk where all of my computer equipment charged up at night. The laptop alone was worth a thousand bucks.

But then something moved right beside me and I realized the guy was not standing across the room about to steal my laptop. He was kneeling on the floor right next to me, pawing through my living-room closet.

There was this strange moment when he blinked up at me in confusion and I blinked down at him in surprise.

I could practically read his thoughts. *Mostly naked man with baseball bat.*

He must have been reading mine. *Burglar on the floor.*

I had just enough time to really look at him. He had pretty hair. Shiny and chestnut brown and pulled back into a bun. There were tattoos creeping up his neck and his eyes were blue or green.

But my moment to observe him was over in a nanosecond when he sprang to his feet. I cocked the bat and stepped toward him, pulling back to swing. It's muscle memory to swing a bat.

My body knew exactly what to do. But halfway through the swing, my gut clenched and my arms went screwy. Because there wasn't a ball at the other end of this swing. It was a person. Yes, a person who had trashed my house, but a person with a pulse and breath in his lungs, standing there in two boots that he'd tied himself before his left his house. A person whose eyes tracked the bat. Who pivoted his body halfway away from me and flinched. The flinch was what really did it. Dogs flinch when somebody is about to kick them. Little kids flinch when a basketball comes flying at their nose. Drivers flinch before a car crash. There was something so . . . heartbreaking about that flinch. He was flinching because of me. Because of the weapon in my hands. Because my two arms were swinging toward him. About to hit him with a baseball bat.

My swing froze midway. I made a sound. He looked up, one forearm protecting his face from me. But seeing me pause was all the time he needed. He reached to the waistband of his pants and something black and metallic flashed in his hand. A bag fell off his shoulder. He was wearing gloves I hadn't noticed before.

There was a handgun six inches from my eyeballs. Staring me down with one cold eye. *You idiot*, that gun seemed to say to me. *You couldn't even swing a bat and now this guy is gonna pull a trigger.*

But he didn't pull the trigger. Instead, he was standing in front of me and then he wasn't. I heard my front door slam. I heard pounding steps on the hallway stairs. And then I was on the stairs, too. On spaghetti legs, in my boxer shorts, I stumbled my way down after him. Was I chasing him? No. Not really. Was I trying to get the hell out of my house? To get help? To get to another person who wouldn't point a gun in my face? Maybe. Probably. Even now it's hard to say.

I found myself in front of the doors to my apartment building, the burglar long gone. *Lou*, I thought to myself. *Lou will help me.* I banged on the door to Lou's apartment but it wasn't the friendly older man who answered. It was a young woman. She had her hair back in a wet messy bun, like she'd showered and just scraped it back afterward. She had on loose pajama pants and a black T-shirt.

I told her I'd just gotten robbed. At that point I didn't even care who she was. I just needed to sit down. I remember she gently pried the baseball bat out of my fingers. I hadn't even realized I was still carrying it.

She called the police, brought me inside Lou's apartment. She dug out some sweatpants and a hoodie for me to wear. I vaguely remembered having seen Lou wear them at some point or another. The woman told me that she was Lou's daughter. That she was taking over his job as the building's superintendent for a while. She brought me a glass of water and sat shoulder to shoulder with me on Lou's couch. We waited for the cops together.

When they finally came, she met them at the front door and then the two of us led them up to my apartment. I answered question after question. Turns out, the guy didn't end up taking much of anything besides the cash he found in the vase. Everything else he'd taken was in the bag he'd dropped before he'd run. My phone and computers were in there. A waterproof Bluetooth speaker I kept in the shower. And that's the one that really got me. He'd even been in my bathroom.

The cabinets in my kitchen were all open. There was even a glass of orange juice sitting on the countertop that I was positive hadn't been mine.

The cops guessed that he thought I was out of town for some reason. There was no reason a burglar would stop and drink a glass of orange juice unless he thought he was totally alone.

I gave them a description of the burglar, told them about the gun. About the gloves. They took pictures and did all sorts of cop stuff. It was dawn by the time they left. Jessie stayed. The cops had told me that I could clean everything up. I didn't need to keep it the way it was for any reason. So, Jessie helped me do that, too. We didn't really talk.

The sun was fully up by the time she stood at the door of my apartment, giving me her phone number in case I needed it for anything. She left, and right as I was about to fix her contact name, my phone rang. It was Detective Cabela. She was assigned to my case and wanted to know if I could come into the precinct later that day.

The next day, I knocked on Lou's door around dinnertime. Jessie answered again. This time I immediately noticed a lot of things I hadn't noticed the first time we'd met. She had a nose piercing and a ton of tattoos. After all my portraiture classes in college, I got used to noticing the way people's faces are put together, and she had a fierce, proud bone structure. Not pretty, not ugly, kind of intense. If I were to draw her, I'd start with rounded lines for her cheeks and forehead and sharp corners for her chin and nose. When she realized it was me at the door, she crossed her arms over her chest and I got a glimpse at her very defined muscles. Her hair was up in that messy bun again and she wore overalls and a tank top.

She looked like Rosie the Riveter.

She looked totally badass.

I held up the six-pack and the chocolate and the flowers and the burritos that I'd bought to say thank you for helping me out.

She'd invited me in and I watched in awe as she cracked open a beer for each of us using only the set of keys she had carabinered to her overalls. I am definitely a bottle-opener sort of guy. She couldn't have seemed cooler to me in that moment. I thought back to the night of the burglary. I burned with humiliation. I'd showed up in my underwear on her doorstep. Weakly clutching a baseball bat I hadn't even had the guts to use. I had cried in her living room. She'd put me in her father's clothes and called the police for me.

I bet she would have singlehandedly beat the shit out of an intruder in her home. I was so embarrassed that I barely made it through that beer. I thanked her profusely, left the gifts, and was on my way.

And then, after that, every time I saw her, I found some way to make a total fool out of myself. She helped oversee the installation of my new security system. What had seemed totally reasonable when I was on the phone with the salesman then seemed like complete overkill in front of Jessie. I couldn't help but wonder what she thought of me. The guy who didn't even swing a bat to defend his own home but was now spending thousands to install a *Mission: Impossible* security system.

A week or two later I stood on the curb by our apartment building and admired a motorcycle that was parked out front. And then there came Jessie, a helmet under her arm and this tiny little smile on her face. She slung one leg over the motorcycle and couldn't have looked more badass.

I awkwardly waved and tripped over the curb. Great.

Some time after that she came around with an exterminator to lay down some mousetraps. Before they left my apartment we all heard a trap snap from my kitchen. She must have seen the horror in my eyes at the thought of cleaning up a mutilated mouse carcass because with that little smile on her face she turned and walked into the kitchen, took care of it herself.

And then, of course, the light bulb debacle.

This whole time, she knew it was me. This whole time I was

teasing and flirting with her, she knew it was Eliot Hoffman, scaredy-cat moron.

This, my friends, is why there was likely a dash of horror on my face when I rounded that corner and realized that JD was Jessie. Generally, you don't especially want to start out a relationship with someone by showing them your worst qualities.

We were literally just talking about being fantasies to one another. Gigi Hadid and The Rock. I'd firmly believed that I wasn't building her up as a fantasy because she was a she-blob in my head. And what kind of fantasy is that?

But now, I think she might have been right to ask me that. Because even though I wasn't dreaming of her being a supermodel of some kind, I was thinking that she probably thought of me as a charming, interesting guy at the very least. I, almost always, make a first impression as someone friendly and fun. I'm not Brad Pitt, but I'm not terrible-looking. I thought there was a reasonable chance of her being into me. But now? Honestly, I can't even think of it without cringing.

We've come a long way together, but is there any chance that she doesn't still think of me as a twerp?

"And why," Frida asks from beside me, "did she run away from you?"

My brain is on the fritz. I can't think in a straight line. I'm still humming with adrenaline from figuring out who JD really is. I'm cringing with embarrassment and discomfort from the resurrection of that most horrible night. I'm stunned and confused and . . . yeah.

"Um. I'm not sure," I tell Frida. Because it's pretty much true.

I've imagined meeting JD about a thousand times and I never once pictured her going white as a sheet and literally sprinting away from me.

Frida is saying something else to me, but I'm not listening. "Sorry to run, Frida," I tell her.

Just a few minutes later I'm closing the door to my apartment and looking down at my blank phone.

No calls. No messages. No nothing.

I kick off my shoes and collapse on my couch.

"She saw me." I hold up my left hand. "And ran." I hold up my right hand. I look back and forth at my two hands as if they could somehow help me figure out what she was thinking. My hands drop.

"She saw me. I said her name. She realized I knew who she was. And then she ran." I press at the space between my eyebrows and get up for a glass of water. "She ran," I tell the inside of the kitchen cabinet as I pull out a glass. "She ran," I tell the running faucet. "She ran," I tell the glass of water before I drink it to the bottom and set it in the sink.

I pull my phone out of my pocket and bring up JD's number. I call her. Just like I expect it to, the call goes straight to voicemail. I realize it's the first time she's ever not answered my call because I've never heard her voicemail message before.

"Hey, you got Jessie. Try again later."

There's her name. In her voice.

Ugh. She literally ran to get away from me. I hang up without leaving a voicemail.

I feel sick. Unfortunately, I recognize the feeling that's icing over the pit of my stomach right now. It's the exact same feeling I had when I woke up in Vegas, right before I realized I was a newly married man. This is the feeling of me realizing that I've just screwed up something incredibly precious and important but I'm not exactly sure how.

I won't pester her. She's a woman who lives in my building who didn't want me to know who she was. This isn't a movie.

Waiting outside her door would only be menacing and weird. First things first, she needs to feel comfortable in her own home. She sprinted away from me on the street.

I have to show her I won't push. I will give her space.

I bounce on the balls of my feet. I'm nervous and uncomfortable because that course of action also gives her so much room for misinterpretation. She sprinted away from me for reasons I either don't know or don't understand. Now that she's not answering my calls, the only thing she'll have left of *us* is whatever that reason is. I don't want that mysterious reason to get bigger than . . . us.

I go to my work desk and sit down, taking a deep breath. I've never sent her a text before because texting is the bane of my existence and I almost always end up misspelling something and then I feel stupid. But I don't want to pester her with another call. And I don't want to send her a voice message about this. I want it there, on her phone, in stark, readable letters. Like a contract. From me to her. I want her to be able to go back and look at it as many times as she needs.

I peck away at my phone. I'm sweating by the time it's done. I go back and read each word independently, checking for any mistakes. Jessie. I don't know exactly what is going on. But I take it you want space from me. I will never bother you. I won't make things awkward for you around the building. But I will be here if you ever change your mind. Apartment 5D. You have my phone number. Please, if you ever want to talk, just call or stop by. My door is always open. Hopeful until then, Eliot. Figuring it's all I can do, I send the text.

Chapter Nineteen

Jessie

I'm throwing one leg over my motorcycle, my palms on the handlebars, when I realize my hands are shaking.

He knows, he knows, he knows. The words are taunting me in the same rhythmic wuh-*wump* wuh-*wump* wuh-*wump* of my heartbeat.

I step back off my motorcycle and take two steps toward the building. I have to go back. I have to talk to him.

But no. I'm pacing back toward the bike. My first instinct was right. I have to talk to Jack first. It's too soon for Eliot to know who I am. I can't go to him, hat in hand, without being able to explain who my brother is. And I can't explain who my brother is without first telling my brother I'm going to do that.

My first instinct was right. Get the hell away from Eliot and find Jack.

But I'm in no condition to weave my way through traffic on a motorcycle right now, so I jog three blocks down to the subway.

The trip to Queens takes a stupid amount of time, because apparently whoever designed New York City's subway system assumed that anyone leaving Brooklyn could only possibly be wanting to head into Manhattan. It's nearly impossible to go north from Brooklyn or south from Queens. But tonight I'm glad for the extra time, because it's given me an hour to practice my speech in my head.

Jack, I need your help, I'll say. *There's this man in the building who I think I'm going to try to date.*

And then I'll describe Eliot.

Jack will figure out who I'm talking about and he'll realize what's about to happen. That two parts of his life are about to collide. He'll tell me everything that happened all those months ago and we'll come up with a plan together.

I get off the train and walk the ten blocks until I'm standing out in front of Jack and Trent's apartment. My heart is pumping water again. I feel weak and energized all at once. After this conversation, I could be leaving here and heading straight to Eliot's door. In a few hours I could be pressing Eliot's doorbell. *Here I am,* I could say to him. *Here's everything I am.*

"Jess?"

I jump. Jack is heading toward me from down the block. He's in his uniform from work and his face is lined with fatigue.

"Hey! You just getting off work? It's so late," I say.

"Nah. I went to the care facility and had dinner with Pops."

My heart squeezes. For all the trouble Jack has caused in the past, he's a good son.

Jack lets us into the house and almost immediately collapses onto the couch.

"Grab me a beer?" he calls.

I veer into the kitchen and grab one for him even though I wish he wouldn't drink during the workweek. He doesn't usually have just one. His eyes are closed when I come back into the room and I sneak over and press the cold can against his ear. He jolts and swats at me, grinning the same grin he's had since we were kids.

"You look a little wrecked," I tell him a moment later as I settle into the armchair and really get a good look at him. He's got bags under his eyes and he's overdue for a haircut.

"Yeah. I've been dealing with some stuff." He takes a long drink and closes his eyes again.

"What stuff?"

He cracks an eye. "None of your business, kiddo."

"Kiddo? I think you forfeited your right to patronizing nicknames when I peeled your ass off of Tasha's floor and dragged you back here."

He winces. "Yeah. Sorry about that."

"What stuff?" I prod again, this time with a pit in my stomach. All the fizzing nervousness and excitement from Eliot seeing me on the street is starting to sour.

"Nothing. It's nothing. I'm gonna be fine." He's waving a hand in the air, trying to change the subject, but all I can see is a man holding on by his fingernails. On closer inspection, his uniform—a gray blue jumpsuit with the name of the electric company embroidered on the breast pocket—is looking almost as tired as he is. My stomach drops.

"Jack, you gotta tell me what's going on. Is everything okay at work?"

"Oh, my God." He leans forward and sets the can of beer on the coffee table with a little too much force and some of it slops over his knuckles. "Yes, Jess. My precious job is fine. I'm not going to do anything to fuck with Pops's health insurance, all right? I've got it covered."

"That's not what I—" I cut myself off, because honestly, that *is* what I meant. He's not fine. It's clear he's going through something, but it's not his welfare I was asking about. Guilt has me dropping my eyes, scraping a hand over the back of my neck.

It's Pops who's been at the forefront of my mind for the last year. Ever since his diagnosis. It's Pops who I've turned my life upside-down for. And I expected Jack to do the same. He looks like he's holding on by his fingernails? Well, aren't I the one who's been expecting him to do just that? Have I cared at all what he's been doing in his free time as long as he shows up for work?

"Jack," I try, "if you need help with something, all you've gotta do is ask."

He frowns at me. "I've got it covered, Jess. Now, is this just a social call? Or did you need something? Because I'm tired and I gotta get up early."

And I just can't do it. All the words get jammed up in my throat and my plan suddenly seems so stupid. If I'm being honest, I knew it was useless even before I got on the train. Unless Jack magically has a time machine, there's no fixing this. The bottom line is this: if Eliot finds out who Jack is, Jack's life goes to hell. And so does Pops's. And so does mine.

Either I tell Jack what's going on with Eliot and make him feel like shit over something he can't change any better than I can. Or I keep my mouth shut and we both just keep individually weathering this terrible time.

"I . . . I just wanted to see your face," I tell him, standing up.

It isn't until I'm on the train again that I let my head fall into my hands. I've been fooling myself into thinking that there was anything I could do. But there's not. It is what it is. I can't be on Eliot's side. I made my decision on that first phone call when I didn't tell him who I was. I'd already betrayed him even then. I chose Jack.

I come above ground in Brooklyn and my phone chirps in my pocket. It's a message from Eliot that he sent an hour ago when I didn't have service. I nearly take a thumb off hastily unlocking my phone. I'm surprised to see that it's not a voice message. It's a text. My first ever from Eliot.

My eyes blur with tears halfway through reading it and I stop, lean against the brick side of a bodega, and try again. "Hopeful," this text says. Hopeful. It's a word that fits him so perfectly, it could be his middle name. He's in his apartment right now feeling hopeful. Even after I ditched him on the street, he's thinking the best of me. He still wants me.

But how would he feel if he knew the choice I've made? How would he feel if he knew that I've decided to make his world a little worse just so I can make mine a little easier?

Hopeful. The word haunts me every step of the way home.

Chapter Twenty

Eliot

It's been days since I've talked to her. But I saw her on the street the day after learning who she was. She'd been standing in front of our closest bodega talking to one of our neighbors. I would have backtracked and avoided them but she caught sight of me, so instead I just awkwardly waved and went past. The expression on her face was . . . I don't know.

Shortly after that I uploaded the next chapter of my webcomic and spent a stupid amount of time deciphering the comments in the hours afterward. Could she have left a comment of some kind? A code for me to decipher? What would her username be? Could she be happypants2018? Probably not. Or what about justiceforbuffy?

I'm guessing no.

A few days after that I ironically found myself in the middle of dispensing romantic advice to Fred. I warned him that I'm a fraud and an amateur and no one should ever listen to me in matters of the heart, but he was insistent. Apparently he's been flirting with a cute girl through a customer service hotline and he needed help with what to do next.

"Be honest," I told him. "Tell her everything. Don't keep secrets because you think it'll improve your chances."

What I don't tell him is that even if he's completely honest and shows her pretty much everything, this woman he has a crush on is still a living, breathing, complex person who lives within her own complicated brain and is guided by her own complicated heart and getting to know someone is almost impossible.

I know, I know, nihilism is not a good look on me.

In the middle of the week I got a disturbing message from my sister. She wanted to know if I'd been part of a joke gift my parents had given her over Christmas. They'd gifted her this stupid shirt that basically called her a quitter. When she asked me if I'd been part of that gag gift, I realized that I might be dropping the ball on this whole brother thing. There's no way in a million years I'd ever want her to think I'd give her something as insulting as that.

The expo she's participating in is coming up on Friday and Saturday, and I realize that I need to make an effort for her. So, come Thursday afternoon, I pack a bag and head to Jersey. She doesn't need to face down our parents alone the night before the biggest professional engagement of her life.

The drive is trafficky, but almost meditative for me. I concentrate on the cars around me, the route, and for once my brain doesn't obsessively track back to Jessie. Of course, once I park in my parents' driveway, I immediately check my phone, see absolutely nothing from her, and I'm plummeted back into the world of *Why*. It's the name of the planet I've been living on. I'll make sure they carve that word on my tombstone. *Why* is the worst word in history. It's an asshole stalker and won't leave me alone. Sure, it's cute if you're in the middle of reading a mystery novel. Or halfway through a movie. When you can be certain that all of your *whys* are about to get turned into *ohhhhhs*. But right now, all signs point to never understanding Jessie. And I just have to make my peace with that and move the hell on.

I have to come back to earth. Where the people who love me and need me live. Like my sister. I take a deep breath, grab my stuff from the backseat, and head inside.

As I quietly kick off my shoes in the foyer of my childhood home, I can hear my mother gently nagging Vera in the kitchen. As she always does, Vera is joking back at my mother. Teasing her, lightening the mood, deflecting the seriousness, never showing how much my mother's attitude hurts her.

When I step into the kitchen, a smile on my face and a six-pack of beers in my hand, I decide I've definitely made the right choice to show up in Jersey. Vera's expression makes the whole thing worth it. She looks like she was seconds away from drowning and I just tossed her a gigantic rubber ducky. She practically launches herself across the room at me.

Vera and I grab the beers and head down to the basement together, which hasn't changed a lick since we were kids. In fact, I'd bet twenty bucks that there's still a half-watched *Die Hard* VHS in the VCR right this very second.

We plunk down on the side-by-side beanbag chairs.

"So, this is unexpected," she says.

I can't help but wince. There's no censure in her tone, but it would almost be easier if there were. "I wish that weren't true. I wish you'd been able to just assume that I'd be here to support you."

I pause for a minute and consider telling her everything. That I'm really just a kid in a grown-up's body. That I'm constantly one second away from screwing everything up in my life. That I've been trying to juggle everything perfectly and to my absolute and utter horror, I've just realized that Vera's one of the things that's slipped through my fingers. I want to tell her that everything she's going through with Mom and Dad—the skeptical expressions, the passive aggressive needling, the constant underlying doubt—that I went through all of that, too.

We talk for a minute about Mom and Dad, but before I can figure out how to steer the conversation in the direction I want it to go, her phone starts ringing. She digs it out from her pocket.

She makes a big show of frowning, but there's a flash of vulnerability when she sees who's calling. My stomach drops. It's definitely a dude who's calling her right now. Vera has, let's just say, *interesting* taste in men. Which is why I've tried so hard to set her up with Fred. She just needs to meet someone who doesn't hide most of himself from her. She needs someone as genuine as she is. "Uh-oh. Who's the guy?"

She glowers at me. "Ugh! When did you become all-knowing? It's annoying!"

"Oh, crap. So it really is a guy? Vera, no!"

"What's wrong with me getting a phone call from a guy?"

"It's not the phone call that's the problem. It's your taste in guys."

"What's wrong with my taste?"

"You have a proclivity for fuckboys."

"I do not! I . . ." She sags, apparently deciding that this argument isn't worth the energy. "Oh, fine. Yes, in the past I've been attracted to fuckboys."

"In the past? So this guy *isn't* a fuckboy?"

"Wellllllll."

"Oh, Vera."

"He's definitely the best guy I've ever had a crush on. He's sweet and supportive and a good listener."

I'm instantly suspicious of these descriptors. If he was this perfect, then she wouldn't be sitting in the basement making excuses about him to me. She'd be upstairs, swinging her feet on her bed and playfully telling him to hang up first. "Then why did you just reject his phone call?"

She looks chagrined for all of half a second before she's blinking up at me from under big eyelashes and pulling a *don't kill me* expression. "Well, he's got this thing called a girlfriend."

"Vera!" If I could wrestle her phone out of her grip right now, I'd put the whole thing down the garbage disposal. Phones are the enemy as far as I'm concerned. They've got both of the Hoffman siblings careening toward heartbreak. They should be considered heavy machinery. Vera and I need a license for these things.

"It's not my fault! You can't control who you have feelings for. And it's not like anything is gonna happen."

She's right. All of that is right. Lord knows I've learned that the hard way. But that doesn't mean she's not waltzing her ass right into a train wreck.

"Seriously!" she insists. "That's why I'm avoiding him right now. Because I'm trying to get over him. That way I can be a good friend and be happy for him and his perfect girlfriend."

"You're avoiding him so that you can get over him?"

"Yup."

"Are you dating anyone else?"

"No, but say, that's a good idea. Why don't you set me up with Fred?"

"I know you're joking, which is the only thing that's keeping me from strangling you right now. Your timing is unreal. Fred's finally taken."

"*What?* Fred, my sweet, sweet destiny, is dating someone? How *dare* he?"

"No, he's not dating her. He's just really into her. It's a long story."

For a moment, I think about all the other long stories I have for Vera. I didn't used to be a secret-keeper. But now, I've got so many things that I'm not talking to anyone about. But we're sitting here, in our musty, familiar childhood basement, and maybe I should just tell her. She's sitting in her beanbag chair the same way she's always sat in it. Completely surrendered to gravity. I know from experience that she'll struggle for a full fifteen seconds to get out of it. She's the same sister she's always been and maybe I've been doing myself a disservice keeping all these secrets from her.

I want to tell her that six years ago I got drunk and married in Vegas and lost one of my closest friends. I want to tell her that I changed my entire life so that nothing like that would ever happen again. I want to tell her the reason I plan all my meals out for the week is because my deepest fear is that if I screw up one thing, I'll screw up everything. I want to tell her that I'm the creator of a very successful digital comic and that a huge part of me wants to quit my job to work on it. I want to tell her that I would have already quit my job to do it full-time if I hadn't gotten drunk and married in Vegas all those years ago. That maybe, for me, having my shit together is more important than my dreams. I want to tell her that I got robbed a few months ago and I haven't slept well since. That I've been falling in love with someone and I tried so hard to make it perfect only to realize that it was doomed from the beginning.

I want to tell her that everything in my life feels like it's connected, one thing bleeding messily into the next, only I can't figure out how it all fits together. That if I could just decipher it, I might have a shot at fixing it. But looking at my life right now is like trying to read for me. Everything flips around on the page. Backwards and upside-down and hiding in plain sight.

"Vera," I say. "I've gotta tell you some things."

But she's frowning at her phone again. I can tell she's not listening to me. Her lip is bitten between her teeth and she struggles up out of the beanbag just like I knew she would. "I'm actually gonna take this call."

"Stay strong." I sound like a sarcastic asshole when I say it, but I actually mean it.

Vera's gone long enough that I finish my beer and then I, too, struggle up out of the beanbag, not any more gracefully than she had. But suddenly I really don't want to be the guy sitting alone in his parents' basement drinking beer. I head upstairs and scrounge around in the fridge, smiling at the same neatly stacked tupperwares of leftovers that are almost always there. Without even opening them, I know I could find my mother's mushroom chicken, a container of mashed potatoes, and a side of green beans. Because it's Thursday night, and that's what my mom always makes for dinner on Thursday nights.

I hear a noise from the living room and realize that Vera is in there, but she's not on the phone. Instead, she's burritoed into one of my mother's Snuggies and staring at her phone. I don't mean to snoop, but as I get closer to the couch, a word on the screen unexpectedly jumps out at me. I'm used to words being a jumbled mess, but clear as day, for just a moment, there's a name I recognize.

I squint. "Wait a second. Who is that email from?"

Apparently she didn't know I was standing behind her because she jumps about a foot in the air. I grab her phone and squint at the screen.

"Hey! Buttwad! Give that back."

Vera tries to sneak-attack me over the back of the couch, but gets tangled up in the Snuggie. I step back and make sure I'm reading this right.

"Damn it!" she shouts. "This is stupid—I'm serious. Give. Me. My. Phone."

Once I know for sure I'm seeing this correctly I can't help but laugh. This can't be true. Pieces fall into place from all over my life. Some people have all the luck. "This is the guy, Vera? Your newest fuckboy?"

"GIVE. ME. MY. PHONE."

She's free of the Snuggie and her fists are doing a great impression of lawnmower blades. She'd haymaker me if I let her, but luckily my big-brother muscle memory kicks in, and I plant a palm on her forehead, keeping her well out of the danger zone.

"Vera, can I ask you something?" I need to clear up a thing or two here. "Did you ever Google Fred?"

She ducks under my hand, emerges in hissing fury inches from my face and attempts to put me in traction as she grabs for the phone.

"Vera. God! Just quit it a minute and answer my question!"

She sags back against the couch, glaring at me. "No. I never Googled Fred. Why would I? I knew I was never going to date him."

I can't help but scream with laughter. Seriously. Some people just have ALL the luck.

She's looking at me like she wants nothing more than to get her hands on a voodoo doll of me. "You look like a psycho right now. Give me my phone!"

This is the only fun I've had in a week. I'm not letting go of this opportunity. "Let's go to his Wikipedia page, shall we?"

"I'm literally going to kill you. Not to sound like a nineties movie, but say your prayers, you twerp! Wait, why does he have a Wikipedia page?"

I search it on her phone. "Here we are. His page. I'm going to show it to you and you need to promise to look. Don't just rip the phone away."

"You will truly be lucky if you see the sunrise."

I palm her forehead again, because someday I'd like to have children and I don't trust her not to kick me in the jewels right now. I turn the phone to show her. She squints at the screen and then immediately looks like her brain has short-circuited.

I figure I might have to explain. "I call him Fred. Because I met him at work and he goes by Frederik or Fred at work. But in his personal life? He goes by his middle name."

I can clearly see that she had absolutely no clue that the man who just emailed her, the man who she was just talking to on the phone, is my best friend, Fred.

"Eliot. Give me my phone."

I blink at her. She does not seem shocked or joyous or amazed. I immediately drop my hand from her forehead and hand the phone over to her. I may have miscalculated this.

"Wait. Crap. Vera, I didn't think you'd be this upset. It seemed funny to me, but . . ."

"Cal is *Fred*."

"Yes—"

"He lied about who he was?"

"No. Well—"

I track back to my conversation with Fred earlier in the week. About the cutie he's been talking to through the customer service line of his company. *Be honest*, I told him. And my guess is that the email she hasn't opened yet contains every bit of that honesty. Unfortunately, my nosy ass got in the way in the meantime.

"Why the hell is he masquerading as a customer service representative!?"

I've really got to do some damage control without further inserting myself in their business.

"He wasn't trying to be deceptive—"

"This entire time I've been talking to the *CEO* of the company!?"

"Really, Vera, he was trying to—"

"Don't talk right now!"

She's got her *I-mean-business* face on and I know from experience that she definitely, you know, means business.

"Let me just—"

"Eliot!"

"Say one more—"

"I swear to God."

"Read the email, Vera."

"How do you know what's in the email?"

"He's one of my closest friends! I helped him—"

"This is *sick*. This is next level. Even for you. Tell me the truth, did you know? Did he?"

"What? No! Vera, I'm not a good actor. Do you honestly think I had *any* idea before the last five minutes?"

She deflates, looking defeated and confused and shocked. And honestly, I can't blame her. In fact, now that I think about it, I don't even know why I thought she would be anything but that. I know exactly how it feels to have someone's identity abruptly revealed to you. To not expect them to be who they are. To develop feelings for someone and then have to reconcile the fact that they've hidden themselves from you.

Oy. For a moment, I see on Vera's face exactly what must have been on mine this entire past week. I can't get further involved. But I can't leave things like this, either.

"Read the email. Seriously."

I have to trust in my best friend to fix this for Vera. I can do nothing more right now.

Vera disappears down the basement for privacy and I plop into her vacated spot on the couch. I eye the discarded Snuggie for a minute and then shrug it on. For a moment, the world hugs me, and I let out a big sigh.

Jessie's got secrets.

Jessie wants space.

I miss Jessie.

I laugh into my palms. I can't believe that after years of failing to set Fred and Vera up on a blind date, they anonymously fall in love with each other through a customer service call.

Does this count as an Eliot fail or an Eliot success story?

There is only one person whose opinion I'd trust on this matter and she still hasn't responded to my text from last week.

I wish . . . but no.

I wish . . . but that's a bad idea.

I wish . . . seriously, Eliot. Just stop.

If only there were a way to tell her how I feel without forcing myself into her life.

Something occurs to me and I try to spring straight up, but I am promptly strangled by the Snuggie. No wonder Vera was having so much trouble attacking me initially. These things are just a fleecy straitjacket. I finally free myself and slump over, hands on my knees. An idea has just rocket-launched itself out of my brain. It's an idea so satisfying and exciting that I wouldn't be surprised to look down and see eight inches of air between my feet and the ground.

I've suddenly realized a non-intrusive way to communicate with Jessie. A way to reassure her of my feelings but give her space all at once.

It's brilliant, it's ridiculous, it finally gives me something to do with all this restless energy.

I have the sneaking suspicion that I might actually sleep well tonight.

Chapter Twenty-One

Jessie

Here's the thing about me. Some people, when they're incredibly sad, kind of lose their ambition. That's not me. In the days after everything with Eliot explodes, I become a productivity monster. And when I say monster, I mean it. The couple in 3F almost scream when they open the door and see me standing there with my toolbox, ready to help them hang shelves.

"You got here . . . fast," the man says.

I grunt. He's surprised to see me, considering he called to ask about hanging the shelves no less than forty-five seconds ago. He doesn't know that I absolutely refuse to be idle right now. He doesn't know that idleness means thoughtfulness and my new life's goal is to never think again. I hang the shelves perfectly, in under fifteen minutes, and then I stand with my hands on my hips in the middle of their living room.

"Got anything else that needs my attention?" I ask.

The couple stands with their arms around one another, their eyes wide. She's about two inches taller than he is and they're wearing T-shirts for the same band. There are framed editions of *Rolling Stone* on their walls. They're really cute together. I hate them.

"Nope!" the woman chirps. "We're all good. Thanks for the help."

I don't blame her for wanting to get me out of her house. I'm well aware that there's a black cloud of rage and disappointment and sadness hanging out over my head. I take the hint and go. Luckily, 6B calls because their hardwood floors are rotting away in places and they've finally decided to do something about it.

I take my storm cloud and spend the day up there. But then, of course, nighttime comes. And suddenly the entire world is the same exact color as my storm cloud and I'm surrounded. Can't see through it, can't step through it, can't get to the other side, nothing to do but just sit there and stew.

I know it sounds crazy, but before Eliot, I genuinely didn't mind staying up late at night. It was soothing to me. Calm. Like everything just sort of slid into slow motion and nothing else was expected of me for the time being.

But since Eliot found out who I am, the nighttime has been when my thoughts have caught up to me. When I have to physically stop myself from going into our text strand and reading his last note to me. It's when I ask myself, over and over, if I'm doing the right thing.

It means that I have to keep busy at night as well. I cleaned Pops's apartment from top to bottom. But there was really only one thing to do after that. And tonight, I'm finally going to do it.

I start at the hardest place. His bedroom. It's already been picked over because he took almost everything he cared about with him to the facility where he lives now. But there are still worn, familiar clothes of his to box up. There are bookshelves with knickknacks to sort through. There are photos of me and Jack that he placed around his room. Boxing and sorting everything takes me two hours. And then the room is bare.

I decide to rearrange the furniture.

By the time I've got everything moved around, my linens on the bed and my own clothes in the dresser, stacks of my to-be-read books lined up under the window, the room is barely recognizable as the one where Pops has lived for so many years.

A lump rises in my throat. This is my room now. I'm not living out of a suitcase anymore. I'm not sleeping on the couch anymore. I'm officially moving in, I guess. Because Pops is not going to move back in. This is my apartment because it's not his anymore. This is my job because it's not his anymore.

I pull out my phone. It's the middle of the night, so I know he won't answer, but that's okay. I leave Pops a voicemail anyhow.

"Hey, Pops. Just thinking about ya. I hope you're sleeping right now. Just finished moving my stuff into your room. I know, I know, I should have done it a long time ago. I guess I just wanted to let you know that . . . I like it here. Doing this job. Living here. You don't have to worry that I don't like it. It fits me . . . Okay, well. Talk to you tomorrow. Sleep tight."

I hang up the phone. For the first time since I moved down here to take everything over, I want it. I want it all. I want this apartment. I want this job. I want to be here in this neighborhood, taking over for Pops, boxing with Raoul, occasionally, hopefully seeing Eliot every once in a while.

I fall face-first into the bed and sleep for a few hours. When I wake up, it's past dawn, and I immediately check my phone. But of course, there's nothing from Eliot. He's not going to push me. He's not going to invade my privacy. I almost wish that he would. If he was just a little bit of an asshole, then I might be able to see him and interact with him without having to make the tough decision to do it myself.

"Just bully me a little bit," I say to my phone, pretending it's

Eliot's face. "Just force me to hang out with you. I miss you, you sensitive, caring jerk."

I jump when my phone rings in my hand. I know immediately who it is. I'm a night owl. He's an early bird. There's only one person on earth who would call me with no reservations at six in the morning.

"Morning, Pops."

"You headed to the gym?"

"Not this morning."

"You were up late last night."

"Yeah."

He pauses for a moment. "What's with the sad little voicemail you left me?"

"It wasn't sad! It was . . . triumphant. Or, it was supposed to be at least. I finally moved you out and took over your room."

The lump that showed up in my throat last night unexpectedly re-emerges, and I sit up in bed, trying to swallow through it. But this time, the tears win. I cover my mouth with one hand as hard, wrenching sobs suddenly make their way out of me.

"Come on, kid. Come on, Jess. It had to happen sometime."

I open my eyes just enough to see tears drip-drip-drop onto the blankets that I'm leaned over.

"Kid!"

"Pops. I gotta call you back."

"No! Don't hang up. Look, you're obviously torn up about something. That guy you told me about? I don't know. But I can hear it in your voice. I've been hearing it all week. I'm calling because I've got something to say to you. You didn't let me say it when you were on the beach. But now you're leaving me voicemails where you sound like your dog just died and now you're crying your eyes out and I really have to make sure you hear it this time, okay?"

I don't say anything, but I don't hang up either and Pops knows me well enough to know that I'm listening.

"Okay. Jessie, I know I've been a good dad to you. I worked hard. I love you. I'm proud of it. But I also know that when your mom left, she took a part of you with her and . . ."

"Pops."

"No. Listen. I think her leaving probably taught you the opposite of what she would have wanted you to learn. Jessie, would you describe me as loyal?"

"Are you kidding? You're the most loyal."

"Would you describe *yourself* as loyal?"

"Well . . . yeah. I learned it from you."

"Okay. Great. That's a good thing to be. It really is. But I want you to know that it was a part of why your mom left."

"Mom left because you were too loyal to her?"

He laughs because he can hear the cardboard sarcasm in my tone.

"She left because I wasn't taking care of myself. I did everything for her. For you. For everyone in the neighborhood. I ran myself ragged in the name of loyalty and I wasted myself away. I changed. I wasn't the man she married."

"Pops."

"She begged me to learn how to take care of myself. But I thought it was selfish. I just kept seeing it as selfish. So, I doubled down and tried like hell to do everything for her. Any little thing I thought she might need. I pushed and pushed. But here's the thing. If you don't take care of yourself, you can't *know* yourself, Jess. And if I didn't know myself, do you think I had a chance in hell of knowing her?"

"What . . . are you saying, exactly?"

"To an outsider, it would probably look like your mother just up and left her caring husband who did everything for her.

Changed her oil, did the grocery shopping. Brought home presents. But the truth is, your mom didn't want any of that. She wouldn't have cared if her car broke down. Or if we didn't have all the right ingredients in the fridge. She wanted me to know her. To sit and listen to her. To talk. She wanted me to recognize that she was unhappy. That she needed help, probably from a shrink or a doctor or something. But I didn't pay attention to any of that. If she wasn't doing well, I took it to mean that *I* wasn't doing enough for her as her husband. I pushed and pushed and called it giving. But . . . that kind of giving, it's the same as taking. There was no space for her in our relationship. In our home. And to top it all off, she always came off as the bad guy to you kids. I was the good dad who showed up with presents and tucked you in at night, and she was the bad mom who cried in the bedroom and disappeared at all hours to God knows where."

"Pops, you're making it too black and white. It wasn't like that."

"I'm making it black-and-white because I need you to see this side of the story, kid. You've only seen one side for so long, and I need to make sure that you see parts of your mom's side, because I think you could really benefit from it right now."

"You think I'm doing the same thing you were doing?"

"Yes. I do. To Jack. You're giving him too much leeway in the name of loyalty."

"No, you don't understand. I'm just trying to make sure he doesn't wind up—"

"Taking responsibility for his own actions? Jess. If he deserves to wind up somewhere, then maybe you should let him wind up there."

"Pops."

"Loyalty doesn't mean making it so nothing bad ever

happens to the person you love. And it definitely doesn't mean sacrificing yourself in the process. Because trust me, kid. If that's the way you show your loyalty to Jack, you're going to end up losing him anyhow. Just like we lost your mom."

"I . . . ugh." I collapse back on the bed in a heap. My eyes are scratchy from sleep and crying. I pull the blankets over my head. The weight of my forthcoming life lies down on top of me. "I don't know if that's what I'm doing or not."

"I'm not trying to tell you to be less loyal to your brother. I'm just trying to say that I hope you're taking care of yourself. And putting yourself first every once in a while. If I'd actually put myself first sometimes, then maybe we would have had a healthier lifestyle at home. Maybe I would have seen that your mom needed serious help. And not just all the little stuff I was doing for her . . . Ah. Anyway. Coulda woulda shoulda. I hope you're good to yourself, kid."

"I'm not . . . bad to myself."

"But you're suffering."

"I'm sad."

"Your whole life is changing."

"My whole life is changing."

"Treat yourself the way you treat me, yeah? Fight to the death for yourself, kid. Just once. At least. Your brother will land on his feet."

When Pops and I hang up a few minutes later, I get up and grab a pen and paper from the kitchen. On the paper I usually use to make my grocery lists, I write down everything I can remember from my conversation with Pops just now. It takes up two sheets of the long, skinny paper, and I put them both under magnets on the fridge when I'm done.

My phone dings and it's one of the tenants needing my attention. That's okay with me. I'm grateful for the stuff to do. I get ready for work and spend half the day up in 6D again, finishing their floors. The rest of the day I'm running errands for the building, picking up potted plants for our front steps and rodent traps for the alley out back.

I don't stop thinking about my conversation with Pops the entire time. He's right, I think. I've spent so much time taking care of other people that I have absolutely no idea how to take care of myself.

Eliot was good for me. But anything good for me feels selfish. And how screwed-up is that? Anything that's good for me feels selfish.

The happiest I've been in years was talking to Eliot on the phone and I wasn't even showing him who I am. I couldn't even give myself the gift of telling him my name.

After work, I shower off, pull on some sweats, put my hair in a wet bun, and sit down with a sandwich. I get a notification on my phone, and my heart swoops when I realize that it's telling me that Eliot's webcomic has updated. The last one was just a few days after he found out who I was, and it was the most wonderful torture to get a peek inside his mind, his world, his art. I wanted nothing more than to talk to him about the turn the characters had taken. But, of course, I didn't give myself that gift.

I'm starting to sense a pattern here.

I open up the app and start in on the next chapter in the webcomic. His story is generally dramatic and thrilling, sometimes creepy or romantic, but it doesn't really matter what's happening on the screen, because whenever I read it, I'm grinning the whole time. There's just something about seeing Eliot's imagination laid out like this that absolutely lights me up on the inside.

I'm halfway through the new chapter when I see something

that makes my heart stop beating. Like, straight up, the blood no longer moves through my veins. A bite of my sandwich plops onto the plate. My eyes are probably bugging out of my head Bugs Bunny style. I put my phone face-down on the countertop and stare at nothing. I pick up my phone and check. Yup. It's still there.

I keep scrolling, see more, and I drop my sandwich completely.

The next few minutes are a blur. Only when I'm straddling my motorcycle, helmet strapped over my wet hair, do I even realize what I'm doing.

There I go, zipping toward stoplights, weaving my way through Brooklyn and into Queens.

Trent is the one who answers the door.

"Jess. Whoa!" He stumbles as I push past him.

"Jack! Jack!"

"Jessie, he's got a girl back there, I wouldn't—"

I don't give a shit. I stride right up to Jack's bedroom door and bang on it with the side of a closed fist.

"What the—Jessie?" There's my dear brother, standing in his open door, his look of confused anger giving way to confused chagrin when he recognizes me. There is, in fact, a girl sitting on his bed. But she's fully clothed and I thank God for small miracles. "What are you doing here?" Jack glances behind him at the girl on the bed. "My sister," he tells her.

I lean around him. "His very pissed-off sister."

Jack closes the bedroom door behind him and leads me into the living room. Trent stands in the kitchen, nosy as ever. I don't care. Let them all hear what I have to say.

I dig in my pocket and pull out my phone. I pull up Eliot's webcomic and shove the whole thing into Jack's hand. "Look. Look at this."

His brow furrows for a moment, but as soon as he registers what's on the screen, his expression clears into amused surprise. "Is this you?"

"Yes." I point at the screen. "This webcomic has tens of thousands of subscribers. It's like, really high on the download charts. People are rabid for this thing."

"Okay . . ."

"And the creator of it *drew me into it*. He created a character out of me. Me! And look. She's totally badass." To my dismay, this morning's tears are creeping up my throat again. I scroll further down to show where the character, named JB in the comic, shows up out of nowhere to karate chop this dumbass character who I, coincidentally in real life, have been wanting to karate-chop for about the last sixteen chapters. And there I am. Drawn into the comic. Nose piercing, tattoos, sloppy bun, work boots and all. In all my glory. I'm a new character.

"Jess, this is cool. But you've kind of lost me."

"I'm pretty sure I'm in love with the creator of this comic. Like *actually*." Trent makes a noise behind me, but I don't care or pay attention. "He's a friend of mine. Someone who I . . . And he *drew me into this world*. This private world he hasn't told anyone about and he . . . What does this tell you, Jack? That he created a character after me?"

Jack looks lost, but he's not a dummy. "Um . . . probably that he loves you back?"

"Probably! Probably, right? I'm in stupid love with this wonderful, gentle, creative, hilarious, kind person, and it sure as hell looks like he's interested." I take the phone and waggle it aggressively. "But I can't do anything about that, Jack. I can't do a fucking thing about that, and you want to know why?"

He grabs the back of his neck and looks apprehensive. "Um. Sure?"

I drop down so that I'm sitting on the coffee table in front of Jack. Our knees hit together and I lean forward and shove at his shoulder so hard, his hand comes up to rub where I hit him.

"I can't do anything about how I feel about him, because you held a fucking gun to his face two months ago."

All the color leaves Jack's face at once.

"I can't even tell this guy how I feel about him because my jerk brother tried to rob his house, put a gun in his face, and fucking traumatized him. What kind of problems are these, Jack? Why the hell are these my problems?"

"Jess . . . I . . ."

I know why he's at a loss for words. Because he didn't even know that I knew the burglar was him.

"He described you to the police, Jack. All the way down to your tattoos. It was my second night as that building's super and you thought it would be a good idea to try and rob one of Pops's tenants? What the hell, Jack? What the hell is wrong with you?"

"I . . . I thought it would be victimless, Jess. When I was there helping Pops move out, I heard some guy talking about how he was going to be out of town and . . . I needed some extra cash. And I must have gotten the apartment number wrong or something . . . I didn't think it was going to be that big of a deal. I didn't want to hurt the guy."

"So, you just broke into his house at night, wanted to steal a couple thousand dollars of his equipment, no big deal. And now this perfectly wonderful person can't sleep at night because someone came into his home and put a gun in his face and you just get to sit there like a total asshole and tell me you thought it was going to be *victimless*?"

"I didn't mean to hurt anyone! You know I'd never hurt anyone in reality. The gun wasn't even loaded."

"Jack, you're such an asshole. Pops's insurance *relies on your job*. You shouldn't be doing anything but waking up in the morning, going to work, coming home, and going to bed. That's it. But you chose to take the opportunity to try and rob one of his tenants? Which, if you'd gotten caught, could have not only gotten you thrown in jail, but could have lost you your job and my job, and potentially gotten me and Pops tied up as your accomplices? How dumb can you be?"

"We're not exactly rolling in money, Jess. I—don't say anything. I know it was stupid. I know it was stupid. I don't even know what I was thinking." He drops his head into his hands and tears at his hair. "I didn't know you were going to fall in love with the guy!"

"Does that even matter, Jack? Does it even matter who loves him? He's a person. Who didn't deserve that shit. You used to be decent. When did that change?"

He's white as a sheet right now and I know exactly why. I've never spoken to him like this before. I've always been his loyal little sister, on his side when he got into scuffles around the neighborhood, helping him move when he got into it with his landlord, leaving a couple hundred bucks around his house so he'd be able to make rent, making him dinner even when he treats me like shit. But right now I'm dragging him by the ear to the principal's office. Poor guy probably has whiplash.

"Nothing's changed, Jess. I'm still me. I just made a mistake." He sees my face and winces. "A really bad mistake."

"And now *I'm* paying the price. And if you get found out, so does Pops. I hope you're happy now that you've made my life so much worse than it had to be."

"Jessie." He grabs my hand and I let him. I'm red-hot angry with him, but I don't want to be cruel. I squeeze his hand, and he squeezes back. "I'm sorry," he says.

"You're not forgiven. I'm mad as hell, Jack. And I will be for a long time. I love you. But you really screwed up my life."

I walk out of the house and straight to my bike. I ride away before Jack can come out and say anything else to me. I need the last word on this one. I really need the last word. I'm floating, I'm churning, I'm dizzy from a sudden loss of weight on my back. I said things I didn't know I needed to say. Half of me immediately wants to take them back. The other half of me wants to engrave them in stone so that I can read them every day. I'm angry and relieved and exhilarated all at once. I'm glad that I have a helmet that covers my face because anyone who saw my face right now would probably think the aliens had officially landed.

I take the long way home, driving through the residential areas instead of down the BQE. By the time I'm parking my bike, the adrenaline from my conversation with Jack has faded and it's replaced with a strange mixture of triumph and resignation. I've done something commendable. I've turned over a new leaf. I won't let my brother's mistakes run my life anymore. And that's a disorientingly freeing feeling. But it also doesn't help my situation with Eliot one bit.

I probably look like that sad Linus meme as I clomp up the stairs to my apartment. I swing open the door and freeze. My fists come up in front of me as I pivot to one side. There's a man in my apartment and in two quick steps I've got him in a headlock.

"Psycho," he gasps. "It's me."

"Oh." I release my brother from the headlock, kick my apartment door closed, and he falls to all fours, coughing and glaring at me. "How did you beat me here?" I ask.

"I don't know. Must've taken different routes."

"You still have your key to the apartment?"

"Yeah. I haven't used it, obviously, in a couple months." He drags himself up to a stand.

"You mean because you didn't want to get caught at the scene of the crime?"

Now we're both giving each other the stink-eye. He breaks first, choosing instead to look around the apartment. "You changed things."

"It's my place now."

"Yeah. Yeah, I guess he's really not going to come back here, is he?"

"No."

We flop onto opposite ends of the couch, and for just a moment, I feel a camaraderie with him. He's 90 percent jerk and makes terrible decisions, but he's also the only other person on earth who knows what it feels like to love Pops the way I do.

"Jess," he says, playing with some of the white strings hanging off the knee of his jeans, "just tell him."

"Tell him what?" I'm still thinking of Pops so I don't understand what Jack is saying at first.

"Your guy. Mr. Baseball Bat. The one you're cuckoo for Cocoa Puffs over. Tell him it was me."

I blink. Jack blinks. The world blinks. I blink again.

Jack throws his hands in the air. "Don't give me that look!"

"Have you lost your marbles? I can't tell him what you did. If you lose your job—"

"There's something else I have to tell you."

"What?" Dread trickles down my spine.

"I've been talking to Sherry."

"Who is Sh—you've been talking to *Mom*?"

He winces and goes a little pale. That's been happening a lot for him tonight. "Yeah. I found her about a year ago."

"How?"

He grimaces. "Facebook."

I blink. He blinks. This time we laugh. "Wow."

"I know. We've been talking a little bit. That's . . . that's what was going on the other night when you came over and I was such a dick. I'd just gotten off the phone with her. She's been helping me a lot, actually. I kind of hit rock-bottom a couple months ago . . . as you obviously know. And she's been there for me. But sometimes it's still hard to talk to her. Sometimes it still catches up to me. What she did. Leaving us. It's been a lot."

"Wow."

"I know. So . . ." He's playing with the jean strings again. "Any chance you knew that she and Pops are still technically married?"

Thirty seconds later the static fuzz is starting to clear from my vision, and I can see Jack leaning toward me, snapping his fingers.

"Earth to Jess. Are you astro-planing or whatever they call that?"

"I . . . what did you just say to me?"

"Sherry and Pops are still married. And she's kind of rich now, I guess. She's a real estate agent upstate. She said that if Pops needed it she'd get him on her insurance."

"Insurance. Upstate. Married."

"Yeah. So, anyway. Tell your boyfriend who I am. I'm . . . really betting the farm on the fact that he won't want to press charges against me, because he's gaga for you. But . . . if he does, I'll get a lawyer. And if I lose my job, we'll call Sherry, and hopefully Pops won't be up the river."

"What are the words that you're saying? Literally none of this makes sense."

Jack stands and puts a hand on my shoulder. "It will. Just give it a little time to sink in."

He gets a soda from the fridge and comes back with one for me as well. At least ten minutes pass in silence as we both slowly drink our sodas, staring at nothing.

Finally, I ask a question the only way I can think to ask it. "*Why*, Jack?"

He shrugs. "Cuz I figure one of us should probably take a crack at being happy."

Chapter Twenty-Two

Eliot

"Do not call her."

I glare at the two people sitting across from me at the restaurant. We've just finished dinner and now we're sharing a couple desserts and talking about our lives. Well, my life. It's been five days since I had the epiphany to turn Jessie into a character in my webcomic. I took some vacation off of work and did nothing but draw, edit, eat, and take catnaps. I currently have a cold-pack ace-bandaged to my drawing hand.

The chapter went live this evening and instead of just anxiously prowling my home like an alley cat, I decided to call up Vera and Fred and force them to have dinner with me. And instead of keeping all these secrets locked up in my brain where nobody could see them, I tried something novel and I told both of them the entire story. Starting in Vegas and ending with uploading my webcomic a few hours ago.

I feel like I've been to church. Like somebody just dumped out all the rocks that have been in my shoes. I didn't even know they were there but now I feel like I could jump ten feet in the air if I tried. I should have known that these two would listen to me with nothing but compassion and curiosity. Joyfully crowing over the triumphant parts of my story and calmly listening through the more dubious chapters.

"I'm serious, Eliot," Vera says, jabbing a very know-it-all finger at me from across the table. "Don't call her. I know you're going to go home and you won't be able to handle the suspense so you'll call her and see if she's read the comic yet, but don't do it." Her pointy finger finally relaxes and she immediately channels that energy into polishing off the key lime pie in front of her. "I still can't believe you've been creating one of the most popular webcomics on the internet for years and you never mentioned it. Can *you* believe that?"

That last part is directed next to her, to Fred, who blushes all the way down to his eyelashes when she turns to him. They had their first in-person date after Vera's expo this weekend and apparently things have been going well because they both look so thrilled just to be sitting next to one another that I could almost puke. Fred, however, is still the Fred I know and love and having the full attention of my pretty sister is definitely raising his heart rate.

He winces a little bit at her question. "I, um, actually already knew."

"What?" Vera and I intone at the same time, sounding exactly like the twinsies we definitely are not.

"How did you know?" I demand.

He's glancing between us, looking a little sheepish. "When you left the company to start your own business, I helped wipe all the design equipment they'd issued to you."

I groan and face-palm. "All my initial mock-ups were on there. I totally forgot to delete them."

He clears his throat. "Yeah. But you never directly mentioned it to me so I figured it was none of my business."

"Have you been following it?"

He blushes again and scratches the back of his head. "Um. Yeah?"

"And . . ." I prompt him, rolling my hand through the air.

"And . . . Rowan's out of the picture, right? Shaker's definitely gonna end up with Hertzog?"

I groan and toss my hands in the air. "I'm surrounded by Shaker and Hertzog shippers."

"Oh, my God." Vera leans in, her eyes lit with mischief. "There's a love triangle in your webcomic? Now I have to read it."

"Yeah. But now that I introduced Jessie's character I might have to rethink—mmmph!"

I gape at Fred who—typically a fairly nonconfrontational person—has just lunged across the table and jammed a bite of pie into my mouth.

"No spoilers," he says. "I haven't read the update yet."

He blushes a little more and sits back in his seat, glancing between Vera and me and scratching at the back of his head again.

"Hey, got any more secrets about my brother?" Vera asks him, prodding at his side.

He dips his head and glances up at her, trying to contain his shy smile and failing miserably. "Probably?"

"Hey," I tell him, swallowing the bite as fast as I can. "Don't tell her. Bros before—" I cut off abruptly at the look on Vera's face. "Never mind. Tell her everything, Fred. Save yourself."

He leans in and says something quietly to her and the look on her face morphs from mutinous humor to soft affection.

I can no longer justify my presence as the thirdest of wheels. It's time for me to give the lovebirds some unchaperoned time.

"All right, kiddies." I stand and throw enough cash on the table to cover dinner for all three of us. "Thank you for the confessional. But I'm gonna get home."

I hug them both, give a quick wave, and am out on the sidewalk before Vera catches up to me. "Eliot! Are you sure you want to go home? You could come over and watch a movie. Or I could come to your house!"

I blink at this unusual offer before I realize what my wonderful baby sister is really doing. I told her about the break-in tonight but there was so much ground to cover between the Vegas wedding and the anonymous girlfriend and the webcomic and romantic gestures that we didn't talk about it nearly as much as I'd guessed we would. "BB, really. It's okay. I've been doing a lot better recently. I'm fine to go home on my own."

She bites her lip. "You promise?"

"I promise." I tug her into a hug. "You're a good sister. Now, get out of here and go have fun with Fred." I wince. "But not too much fun. Oh, God. It's just occurred to me that we're only like four blocks from your house. You're totally gonna go back there together, aren't you? Never mind. Don't answer that. Never answer that. Oh, boy. I'm really gonna have to get used to you and my best friend dating. Okay. Bye. I'm going now. I'm going to find the most interesting movie on earth and watch it fifty times in a row. I'm going to pin my eyelids open, *Clockwork Orange* style. That's the only way to get this line of thinking permanently erased from my poor, poor brain."

Vera gets a maniacal glint in her eyes and she opens her mouth, surely to say something I will have to scrub from my memory with steel wool and hydrogen peroxide.

"No!" I shout, shoving my fingers in my ears and leaping away from her. "I'm leaving. Keep your thoughts to yourself!"

She's laughing and waving but I hear nothing as I jog toward my apartment. Because I'm a masochist, I pull out my phone. Nothing. No calls or texts. I pause for a second and go into the webcomic app, just to make sure—for the hundredth time—that everything has been uploaded correctly and yup. Wow. There are already a boatload of likes and comments. I quickly scroll through them and I nearly sprain my cheek muscles when I see what people have to say about the Jessie character I included, named JB in the comic.

Let's just say she's . . . already pretty freaking popular.

I sigh and kick at a sidewalk crack as I shove my phone back in my pocket. Of course people love her. She's incredibly magnetic and interesting and fierce and . . . even better in real life.

I've walked half a block further when I stop still in my tracks. My phone is vibrating against my leg. I nearly rip my pocket off in my desperate attempt to see who is calling.

"It's her!" I shout at the top of my lungs, scaring the pants off about a dozen innocent bystanders. I scramble to answer the call, my big, dumb thumbs barely cooperating. I have no plan, I have no idea what to say, I have nothing but my heart in my throat and zero air in my lungs. But I don't care. Being cool is for the birds. Jessie is calling me. She's calling me. I answer.

Chapter Twenty-Three

"Jessie?! Hi."

". . ."

"Jessie? Hi. Are you there?"

"You called me Jessie."

"Right. Hi. Wow. I'm so glad you called."

"I wasn't sure you even knew my name."

"Oh, God. I . . . well, I didn't. I'm a total twerp, I know. But I forgot it because the night we met was so . . . awful. And then I was too embarrassed to ask again, because we'd been through so much together at that point and . . . oh, boy. This is not going how I wanted this conversation to go."

"How did you want it to go?"

"I don't know. God. I've had all this time to think about nothing but this moment and I still have no idea what I wanted to happen. I just wanted to hear your voice. That's all, really. I've missed your voice."

"So . . . you've completely stolen my likeness for your webcomic."

"You read it? Eek. Sorry. I sound like I swallowed a bug. Let me try again. You read it?"

"I read it. And I'm going to sue you."

"I can't tell if you're joking. That's okay. Go ahead and sue me. Let's make it a really messy, protracted process. That way we can talk every day."

"You don't have a very strong self-protection instinct, you know."

"Trust me—I know. That's why I'm so grateful you were there that night. The night of the break-in. I knew you would kick ass for me, even if I couldn't do it myself."

". . . I was glad I could be there, Eliot."

"Jessie, I have to say something."

"Okay."

"That day on the street—"

"We don't have to talk about that."

"No. I really want to clear something up."

"All right. Go ahead."

"Well, turns out Frida Hawkins was there. She saw the whole thing."

"Yeah. She was pumping me for gossip about it for a few days afterward."

"Me too. Anyway. She came up to me right after you walked away and wanted to know what happened. She wanted to know why there was a look of horror on my face when I saw you."

"Okay . . ."

"And I was confused because I didn't know why my face would show horror when I wasn't horrified. I was shocked, but not horrified."

"You did look a little horrified to see me, Eliot."

"Well, I thought about it more and I realized that maybe there was something like horror there, but not because you were you. But because you were you."

"Oh. Got it. That completely clears everything up."

"Let me explain! Okay, at that point I was pretty much thinking of JD as the coolest person I'd ever met. She was so calm and interesting in this unexpected way. She always knew what to say and always seemed interested in what I had to say. She was down to be silly with me and never made me feel stupid. To be perfectly honest . . . I had a major crush on JD. Like, a major one."

"Eliot."

"But, of course, there was a major roadblock."

"The fact that you didn't know who JD was."

"Exactly. But I liked JD so much that that was starting to seem kind of, I don't know, irrelevant? And then I saw you on the street and put the pieces together."

"And you were horrified."

"Yes and no. I was horrified because, here's the thing—I also happened to think that *you* were pretty freaking cool. Jessie the superintendent, I mean. You might remember from our phone calls, but I actually mentioned you a few times."

"Of course I remember. You were talking about me to me without knowing who I was."

"Right, well, hopefully it didn't pass your notice that I thought my super was competent and badass and—"

"Someone you were always making a fool of yourself in front of."

"*Exactly.* Jessie, when you have a crush on someone, you don't want to be a fool. You want to be, at the very least, able to screw a light bulb in properly. But I was so much less than that. I was the guy who couldn't even defend his own home. I was the guy who'd cried on your couch in his underwear. Like five minutes after I'd first met you. Just the other day, you saw my friend do the limbo under my legs while I did the splits and nearly fell over."

"Yeah, now *that* was special. That was the closest I came to telling you who I was. I just wanted to laugh with you so badly."

"But that's why there was horror on my face, I guess. Not because you were you and I was expecting something different. But because you were you and I was realizing that any chance I'd had at seeming, I don't know, desirable to you was probably out the window. You'd seen me at my worst like fifty times already. I was standing there, just kind of watching everything go up in smoke."

"Eliot . . . those things . . . aren't things that would make me not like you. You're expecting yourself to be this, like, über masculine dude. I don't care if you don't want to hit someone with a baseball bat. Actually, it's really nice that you *don't* want that. First of all, I can defend myself, and you, too, if it came to that. Second of all, men are expected to, like, lust after violence and that's just toxic masculinity at its worst. You're not bloodthirsty? That's great, Eliot, and I'd never ask you to be. You're a gentle person and honestly, that's pretty much my favorite thing about you. As for the light bulbs and the mousetraps, well, these are things that I'm comfortable with. It's my job, you know, to take care of stuff like that. I don't care if those things aren't on your radar. Having feelings for someone isn't about expecting them to be . . . anything, really. It's about *knowing* somebody. And liking them for who they are."

"So—you—are you saying that—all that stuff—me—you—"

"Wow. Deep breath, buddy."

"Are you saying that you have feelings for me?"

"Eliot—"

"Because let me just get this out in the open first, Jessie. I know I was shocked that you were you. But I need you to know that I am so unbelievably *glad* that you're JD. And it took a minute to assimilate all the new information, but now I couldn't picture anyone else being you. And I'm so into—"

"Eliot, wait. Just . . . wait."

"Waiting."

". . ."

"I mean, I'm not waiting particularly *patiently.*"

"Okay. Look. There's something I have to tell you. And if you make me go all squishy on the inside I might not be able to get through it. And if I hear you say that you have feelings for me, I might do the cowardly thing and just . . . Look, I have to tell you, so just listen, okay?"

"I'm listening."

"Where are you right now?"

"I'm just unlocking my apartment door and heading inside."

"Good. Because you should probably be sitting down for this."

"Um. Okay. Just a sec . . . there. I'm sitting in my living room. Bombs away."

"Okay. I'm just going to tear the Band-Aid off. The guy who robbed you? Well, unfortunately he's my brother. His name is Jack. And yes, I knew it was him from the moment you gave your description to the cops. I didn't say anything to you or the cops because, well, he's my brother. And I was trying to protect his dumb ass. Not only because I love him and don't want him to go to jail, but because—"

"Your dad is on his health insurance."

"I . . . yes. Wow, you have really been paying attention to everything I've told you, huh?"

"Everything."

"Okay . . . well. I had no idea what to do. Especially after you and I started talking on the phone and I realized just how much that night was screwing with you. All I wanted was to make you feel better. To get you some closure. To help you feel safe and secure. But I had no idea how to do that without telling you the truth. And . . . selfishly . . . well, I knew that as soon as you knew who my brother was that you wouldn't—we couldn't—that everything would just end. And it's been a really hard year for me. Pops. Moving. Leaving my old job. Starting up here. My jerk brother. Pops. And talking to you made me happier than I'd been in such a long time. I just wanted it to last . . . a little longer. Like I said, it was selfish. I should never have let things go this far. Especially because I knew it was doomed from the beginning."

"Don't say that."

"Which part?"

"The doomed thing. Your brother's actions . . . why do you assume I'd hold you responsible for them?"

"I don't mean that, exactly. I just mean, are you going to come over for Thanksgiving dinner and ask Jack to pass the mashed potatoes after he broke into your house and held a gun to your face and traumatized you?"

"You . . . were thinking about that already? Having me over to spend time with your family?"

"No! I mean . . . yes. But not like that!"

"I . . . don't think I've ever heard you this flustered before. If it wasn't like that then what was it like?"

"When you have a crush on someone you just kind of start to think about the future a little, you know? And all I'm saying is that I really didn't think we could have a future together because of what Jack did. And because I covered for him."

". . ."

"Eliot? Are you still there?"

"I'm here. I just . . . wow. This is a lot."

"I know. I know. And I'm sorry. I'm so sorry for everything."

"Your brother . . . does he do this a lot?"

"No. He's done some stupid shit before. But never anything

like this. I'm not making excuses for him, but I think he was stressed about money and Pops and yeah, there's no excuse. I'm going to stop talking now."

"Does he carry that gun around with him?"

"No. And he says it wasn't loaded if that's any consolation."

". . ."

"Eliot?"

"He's gonna get himself killed if he keeps doing things that stupid. What if I'd had a gun? A loaded one?"

"I know. It makes me sick to think about it."

"You said that he's had some substance abuse problems in the past?"

"Yeah."

"Have you talked to him about rehab?"

"I've been thinking about it."

"Now would probably be a good time. If this isn't rock-bottom for him, well, do you really want to see how much farther down it goes?"

"No. You're right. I just . . . with everything with Pops and this new job, it just sort of . . . I don't know how to go about even having that conversation with him."

"You've had to do everything on your own, Jessie. Take care of your dad. Your brother. All the tenants."

"It's still no excuse. Not when Jack needs so much more help and I can't give it to him."

"You're not failing. I can hear in your voice that you think you are. But you're not. You've got too much on your plate. Let me help, Jess. I'll help."

". . ."

"Are you there?"

"What are you even saying right now? I just told you that Jack is the one who . . . and you're offering to help me?"

"Look, I'm not saying that I want to *see* him right now. Or that he and I will ever be buddies. But it's not like . . . even if he were a complete stranger, I'd want to make sure that he got the help he needed. Breaking into someone's home with a weapon, it's a pretty desperate move. Someone who has all their needs met, they're not likely going to do that."

"You're not going to call the cops on him?"

"Jessie . . . God. No. I want him to get better. To get the help he needs. And he's not going to find that in the criminal justice system. We both know that. The only reason I wanted to get the cops involved in the first place was because I didn't want him to do that to other people. And what other option did I really have? But if you're telling me there are other options . . . if there are other ways to make sure he doesn't do something like this again, then, yeah, I'd rather not get the cops involved."

"Eliot."

"Are you crying? Oh, crap. I didn't mean to make you cry. What kind of crying is this? Sad crying? Happy crying? Relieved crying?"

"Why aren't you judging me? You should be judging me and blocking my phone number."

"I fear I haven't been clear enough about how I feel about you. Do you need to read the webcomic again? I'll wait."

"The *webcomic*."

"No! Crap! I didn't mean to make you cry more! Forget I said anything about that."

"Eliot, maybe I am going to need you to be really clear here."

"Clear about which part?"

"You're making it seem like you're . . . going to be by my side. And if you're not, I kind of need to know right now because . . ."

"I'm not going to let you do all of this alone, Jess. I mean, you get to decide how much you want to share with me. But I'm in. I'll help with anything. Everything. I've learned how to be very organized in my life. We can take it step by step. We'll make a plan for how to help Jack. Step one is probably some sort of substance abuse counselor? Or a therapist? I don't know really. We'll have to research it and figure out what steps to take."

"Stop talking."

"What?"

"Just . . . shhhhh."

"Can I ask a question?"

"I . . . sure."

"Is that the whole problem? The reason why you didn't want me to know who you are? There's nothing else?"

"It's a pretty freaking big problem, Eliot."

"Sure. Of course. I'm just wondering if there is anything else I need to know."

"That's the whole thing. Other than the fact that I was pretty sure I would scare the pretty-boy pants off of you once you found out who I was. But I figured that if you couldn't handle it then you weren't worth the heartache probably."

"Hold on. Back up. Why would you scare my pretty-boy pants off? And, wait. Are you calling *me* a pretty-boy or saying that I wear pretty-boy pants?"

"Both? I've seen your work outfits. You wear, like, khakis. And suits and stuff."

"Okay. Noted. We've already been over the fact that you're cooler than I am. But why would you think you'd scare me?"

"The tats? The piercings? The combat boots? I guess I just assumed I wasn't your usual style."

"Hmm. Jess, any chance that you've looked at the comments for the most recent episode of the webcomic?"

"No. Not yet."

"Well, most of them are about the new character."

"The one I'm suing you over?"

"Yup. That one."

"What do the comments say?"

"Mmm. I believe the most common word used is 'snacc' with two *c*s."

"Um."

"Yeah. There's a lot of tongue-out emojis and people begging the character to step on them."

"The internet is such a stupid place."

"Agreed. But I'm just saying, you think you're not my style? I'm under the suspicion that you kind of might be *everybody's* style, if the comments section is any indicator."

"You really see me like that? The way you drew me?"

"That's the way you are. Exactly."

"Eliot, the character shoots a nail gun and fights three different dudes at once."

"Okay, so I might have inflated your combat skills a little."

"And her cheekbones look like they could poke somebody's eye out."

"I told you you have a fierce face."

"I think you might be seeing me through rose-colored glasses."

"You told me I'm a pretty-boy so I'm willing to bet there are two pairs of glasses involved."

"Do you think the issue is that we're seeing each other inaccurately? Or that we each see *ourselves* inaccurately?"

"Mmm. Good question. Maybe one of the best parts of starting something up with someone is you get to see all your yummy parts through their eyes. Like, I legitimately have been thinking that I was a total loser for how I reacted to the break-in. But then you just described it as me being a gentle person. And . . . that doesn't sound so bad. I don't mind being a gentle person. But it literally didn't occur to me to think of it that way until you mentioned it."

"So, maybe it's my job to make sure you see yourself through my eyes?"

"And vice versa. We'll be each other's selfie stick. Metaphorically."

"That doesn't make sense but you're cute so I'll let it slide . . . oh, my God."

"What?"

"Nothing. I just . . . I'm overwhelmed. I said goodbye to you in my head like fifty times since that day on the street. I never thought . . ."

"I didn't think so either, Jess. I thought you were long gone. I think it's probably obvious, but I'm so, so glad you're not gone."

"I'm definitely not gone."

"So, can I, like, say hi to you in the halls and stuff?"

"No way, loser. I can't be seen with a prep like you."

"Ah. Got it. I totally understand. I need to pull a Sandy from *Grease*. Maybe I'll get a tongue piercing and a leather jacket. Would that help?"

"Frida Hawkins would have a coronary."

"I think she's gonna have a coronary anyhow when she finds out we're dating."

"We're not dating."

"What? Are you kidding me? I basically just pledged my undying devotion to you."

"Yeah, but we've never been on a date. Thus, we're not dating yet."

"Ah. I see. Well, get your shoes on. I'm grabbing my coat. I'll be downstairs in thirty seconds."

"..."

"Wait, someone is knocking on my door. Oh, jeez. JD, is that you?"

"Come and see."

"Holy smokes. I can see you through the peephole."

"I'll give you two hundred points right now if you let me in."

"Two hundred?! This is . . . wow. Give me a second to get my blood pressure under control."

"You were just talking such a big game about picking me up for a date, and now you're too scared to open the door?"

"At some point you'll learn I'm like 80 percent bluster."

"At some point you're going to have to come to terms with the fact that you're a lot braver than you think you are, Eliot."

"Here you are. JD in the flesh."

"Here I am."

"Come in."

Epilogue

Eliot

Four Months Later

"Eliot, honey, you look *terrible.*"

I turn and can't help but grin at Frida's horrified expression as she takes in my appearance. I admit, I've looked better.

It's late summer and I'm standing in the sun, so I'd probably be sweaty even if I hadn't just finished a two-hour workout at Geddy's, but as it is, my clothes are literally soaked. I can see in the reflection of the cookie shop window next to me that my hair is sticking up in every direction and—yup—I'm definitely gonna have a shiner tomorrow. My sparring partner got a little overexcited today.

If you'd asked me four months ago if I'd be comfortable throwing punches in a gym, the answer would have probably been three straight minutes of me laughing. But that's Jessie for you. First she convinces you you've secretly been a badass this whole time, and then she's accidentally popping you in the eye during a workout.

"Oh," I say to Frida. "I was just working out."

She looks less than impressed by my answer. "Where? The sewer?"

I laugh. "No. Over at Geddy's boxing gym."

She raises an eyebrow. "I didn't know you boxed."

"My girlfriend got me into it." The words pop out unexpectedly. Jessie's officially been my girlfriend since about thirty seconds after she came up to my apartment the night we finally reconciled. We've told our families and friends, but not any of the other tenants in the building. And now, Frida's eyes have lit up like I just revealed I'm secretly the prince of a small European country.

"A girlfriend, you say—"

The door of the cookie shop jingles and Frida cuts off when someone comes up behind me and puts me in a headlock. I recognize the constellation of tattoos on the forearm in front of my face. If Frida weren't watching me, I'd plant a quick kiss there because kissing is how I show love. And I do honestly love this forearm, because it's Jessie's and headlocks are one of *her* most preferred methods of showing love.

She must not have seen I was talking to a fellow tenant when the headlocking began, but she's certainly gotten the message now because suddenly we're both standing straight, shoulder to shoulder, like schoolkids caught skipping math class. Jessie wordlessly passes me the double fudge cookie she just went into the shop to buy for me.

Frida's eyes follow the path of the cookie. Her gaze darts from Jessie to me to the cookie and back to Jessie.

She's doing salacious arithmetic in her mind, I can see it. She's preparing to sprint to the top of the building where she keeps her messenger pigeons. In T-minus ten seconds, the entire city shall know that Eliot loves Jessie.

"Girlfriend?" Frida says, a menacing glee in her eyes.

I look down at Jessie and cock my head in question. She's all messy bun, sweaty workout clothes, and that expression that just kills me. Like her face is perpetually saying *I'm in if you're in, Eliot.*

I put my arm around her shoulders and kiss her messy hair. "Girlfriend," I confirm to Frida.

Frida's off and going, words flying out of her mouth at warp speed. Apparently she's got a lot to say about me, Jessie, and, I assume, the cookie. But as the three of us start walking together, I gotta admit, I'm not listening. I'm too busy smiling down at Jessie, who is raising her eyebrows back at me. I tangle my fingers with hers the way I always do when we walk around in public, so that everyone will know that this sweet-hearted little toughie chose *me*.

When we get back to our building, we wave goodbye to Frida and duck together into Jessie's apartment, fingers linked. I spend so much time down here that it's starting to feel a little bit like *my* apartment as well. I haven't brought it up with her yet, but my busy, busy brain has started to wonder what it might be like if all my stuff, ya know, lived with all her stuff. My apartment upstairs hasn't really felt like home in a long time anyhow.

Jessie locks her door and turns and gives me the look. It's my favorite look of hers. It's the one she gave me right before our first kiss. Where her mouth is smirking but her eyes are happy. She takes a big step toward me.

"I'm sweaty," I warn her, but her arms go around my neck anyway.

I grin down at her, getting a kick out of our six-inch height difference the way I always do. In so many ways, to me, Jessie is larger than life. The strongest, the fiercest. She also happens to be a little bit of a peanut and I die for it on a regular basis.

She goes up on her toes, and when her lips touch mine, my entire body goes hot, from the part of my hair all the way down to my toenails. My heart does the fifty-yard dash and I deepen the kiss, my hands in her hair and her familiar, perfect flavor on my tongue.

She breaks the kiss and we're breathing hard, forehead to forehead.

"Eliot."

"Hmm?"

"Frida's gonna tell the whole building."

"It's about time."

"She's gonna be watching our every move from here on out."

"I've been thinking she needs a new hobby anyway."

"There's no going back, you know."

"Who's going back?"

"Nothing scares you, huh?"

"Plenty scares me. But as long as I've got you? I figure I'm safe."

"That's right. I'll protect you."

"Thank goodness for wrong numbers."

"And insomnia."

"Yeah, when we're accepting the award for best relationship ever, we'll definitely have to remember to thank insomnia for its indispensable role in getting us together."

"Oh, Lord. You're gonna draw that, aren't you. The award for best relationship ever?"

"We can put it on the fridge."

"You're lucky I find this cute."

"You're lucky I don't find you intimidating."

"We're both lucky, then."

"We are. We definitely are."

Acknowledgments

To Tara Gelsomino, one day I'll have a marching band show up on your doorstep and then you'll finally have an idea of just how thankful I am to/ for you. For now, just know that I truly mean it when I say thank you for answering my Sunday afternoon texted questions, for gently nudging me when I've forgotten to email someone back, for being the best ideas-bouncer-off-er there ever was. To Allison Carroll, your reaction to this book will be forever in my mind. You allowed me to get excited and ambitious about this story. Before you it was merely a project that I thought was working. You showed me the sparkle. Thank you. To Kate Byrne and Jill Cole and, honestly, the entire team at Headline, I really hit the jackpot. Every day I work with this team is another day that I am grateful to work with this team. What a group of hardworking and positive people. Thank you for your attention to detail, creative vision, and constant professionalism. I am so grateful to you all! To my mom, who has read every word I've written since I was (literally) just learning to hold a pencil, I love you, your constancy has made it possible for me to take the risks I needed to take in order to get where I am today. To my dad who brags about me at any/every opportunity, remember the 10 year plan, you'll reap your rewards then. To my Sands family, thank you for not taking my texting skills personally, for celebrating me, for supporting me, for seeing me. To my Ambro family, thank you for being proud of me and loving me and allowing me to grow up and change. I love you. And lastly, to Jon and Frankie, you two are there each step of the way. Literally. Our evening dog walks are the happiest part of my day, everyday. Thank you for listening, for sharing your lives with me. Our unit is what I am proudest of. I love you.

Read on for a taste of a warm and emotional romance that will tug on your heartstrings . . .

Available now from

HEADLINE
ETERNAL

Chapter One

This baby will not stop judging me.

The B train brakes and we all slide two inches to the side. Perched atop their mother's lap, the straps of a bright red sunhat pinned under chubby cheeks, somber, unblinking eyes, the baby studies me, trying to decide if I have a soul.

I stick my tongue out and make my ears dance.

No reaction.

I pull my cheeks out to the sides and do rabbit teeth.

Not even a blink.

Finally, as the train is pulling into my stop, in a last-minute bid to be judged human, I use my ponytail as a mustache.

And there. Finally. I get one radiant, two-toothed smile.

Thank goodness. I guess there is a soul in this scraped-out husk of mine after all. I wave goodbye and bound up, off the train, and head west. It's dog-breath hot out here and I can't believe I've mustered up the energy for this.

But the thing about losing the person you love the most on earth is—somehow—you still have to do mundane things like tie your shoes and make enough money to continue to exist in this punishing world. So, I plod on. Toward yet another short-term nannying gig. Just to keep the Froot Loops on the table. Even though I'd really rather crawl into that trash can over there and emerge in about a decade.

Oh, look. I'm here. It's a gigantic brick apartment building. The lobby is populated by a group of people who look so happy I wouldn't be surprised if their lives suddenly turned into a musical. They mob the doorman with luggage, so I go up on tiptoes and shout to him where I'm headed.

"Ah. They're expecting you," he calls to me in an Eastern European accent. "Eighteenth floor."

By the time the elevator dings, I'm in a better mood. One of my former babysitting families recommended me to Reese so that I can help out with her kid while she's out of town this weekend. Besides, here in the worst six months of my life, the only thing that's brought me even a hint of happiness has been hanging out with the kids I babysit. I'm between jobs right now, so this new family is likely going to be the only spot of light in my life for a bit.

I ring the doorbell and ten seconds later, perfection personified answers the door. She's got blond hair in a high ponytail and is decked out in head-to-toe Lululemon.

"Hi, I'm Reese." She holds out her hand and smiles so toothily that I find myself grinning back.

"Lenny. Nice to meet you."

"Thank you for agreeing on such short notice. My friend Harper usually helps out for stuff like this, but she's busy during the days this weekend. She's the one who will be staying overnight with Ainsley. Anyways, come in, please. Did you get my email?"

"I did," I assure her. It was literally six and a half pages single-spaced and filled with so much loving detail on how to care for her daughter that it teared me up. I come inside and kick off my shoes, straightening them when I realize that all the other shoes are in perfect pairs. We're in a roomy front hallway, painted a trendy mauve and lined with gigantic black-and-white photographs.

"So, Ainsley is back in the—" The doorbell rings again

right after Reese closes the door, and she frowns. She pulls the door back open and her shoulders cinch about two inches upward when she sees who it is. "What's up, Miles?"

There's a man standing in the crack of the door that Reese has just opened, and I get the feeling he might have wedged his foot in there so she can't close it.

He's not good-looking, really. Low-grade sexy. He's wearing a used-to-be-black hoodie stretched over two big shoulders and faded blue jeans. Viciously short dark hair and the kind of stubble you can't ever shave away. Judging by that promising scowl, he's the type who'd really enjoy partaking in a public bathroom tryst with a near stranger. I can already see it now. He and I will have a tumultuous two-year fuck-fest, defined by me perpetually being sent to voicemail. He'll stand me up on Thanksgiving, thereby dumping me. But then he'll realize horrifically, cataclysmically, that he's been in love with me this whole time. He'll come crawling back to me on all four appendages. I'll make him wait outside my door for a year before I let him back in. Eventually there'll be a ring with a black diamond so dark I can see his soul inside it. We'll get married on Halloween and his wedding present to me will be a sex toy. It sounds ecstatically fun.

It's probably apropos to mention that I instantaneously spin elaborate fantasies about almost every man I ever meet. Not to say that this guy isn't special; I have just fallen in love, after all.

He looks over Reese's shoulder and spots me, his gaze narrowing and his eyes taking me in from socks to eyebrows. I don't think I've passed the test because he leans forward and thus commences an aggressive (and nearly silent) whisper fight between the two of them and it's getting a little icy in here.

I occupy myself with the black-and-white prints for something to do. That's when I realize that what I'm looking at are actually gigantic photographs of someone very famous.

"Sorry about that," Reese chirps at my elbow, and I jolt. I hadn't heard her approach. She's got a plastic smile superglued to her face and when I look back, the man is still standing in the now fully open door, glowering in our general direction.

"No problem," I say, and then jog one thumb toward the portraits. "Big Willie Nelson fan?"

"Hm? Oh! Ha. Willie's great. But that's my dad there next to him. They toured together for a while."

"Oh, wow!" I lean in and sure enough, there's another guy in all the pics, at the mic in some and jamming on a steel guitar in others.

"Carp Hollis," she says, supplying the name I clearly couldn't come up with. "Ever heard of him?"

"Your dad is Carp Hollis?" I don't know much about bluegrass or country, but even I know that he's kinda royalty.

"Yup. That's Dad." She looks affectionately at the pictures before her expression clouds. I instantly recognize that look, and my stomach drops to my toes. "He passed about a year and a half ago. This is his apartment. Ainsley and I are still getting used to it, to be honest . . . Why don't you come meet Ains."

She starts to usher me out of the hallway.

"Reese!" calls the man who is still standing in the open door.

She doesn't turn around. "Then stay if you want, Miles!"

I'm looking back and forth between them. "Um. I'm Lenny," I offer to him with a little wave of my hand. "Lenny Bellamy."

He's ignoring me, staring daggers into the back of Reese's head.

"That's Miles. Ainsley's uncle," Reese finally says into the silence. "He lives upstairs. He'll probably be around today, if that's okay with you."

"Oh, uh. Sure?" I don't usually enjoy babysitting with an audience, but he *is* my future husband after all, as prickly as he may be.

The apartment is gargantuan and curated and polished. Kitchen, living room, dining room, a handful of bedrooms and bathrooms, and then, finally, in what she refers to as the "drawing room," is a little somebody who is, in fact, drawing.

"Ains," Reese calls.

The little somebody doesn't stand, she just drops her colored pencil and pivots on her knees to face us. She's about seven years old, with dandelion levels of staticky hair. Tiny purple glasses magnify her eyeballs to twice their size and she's swimming in a very faded Madonna concert tee. "Is that a cat eating lasagna on your shirt?" she asks me.

"It's Garfield," I clarify.

"Who's that?"

"Oh, it's a good thing we're going to hang out all weekend because we've got a lot of ground to cover."

She nervously tugs the hem of her T-shirt. "Okay."

"I'm Lenny," I say, and I leave the adults behind to sit next to her. "What's your name?"

She frowns at me. "Mom didn't tell you?"

I smile. "She did, but people usually start getting to know each other by exchanging names."

"Oh. Yeah. I'm Ainsley." She makes a puke face.

"You don't like your name?"

"There are three other Ainsleys at my school. Different grades but . . ." She shrugs.

"Oh, really? Wow. Ainsley sounds like a unique name to me. If you could choose any other name, what would it be?"

She shrugs again, still nervous to meet me. "I don't know. Something cooler. Like . . . Blackbeard. Or Darth Vader."

I burst out laughing, and she tries to hide her pleased smile while she plays with the hem of her T-shirt.

I instantly like her, and I like her mom more by extension. This uptown address, Reese's perfect ponytail, head to toe in Lululemon, I would have put some serious money on Ainsley having been carefully manicured into a mini-Reese. I've seen it before. But Reese and Ainsley are a delightfully odd couple.

Reese is leaning in the doorway and smiling at us. "Listen, I'm going to get a little work done in my home office for a bit before I head out. Come get me if you need anything, Ains."

"'Kay."

Reese disappears with a wave and Ainsley does a double take at the doorway. "Oh. Hi, Miles."

"Hey. I'll be around too . . . if you need me."

Ainsley looks instantly confused. "Why would I need *you?*" she asks in that guileless yet utterly gutting way that children have.

For the length of a single camera flash Miles looks mortally wounded. But then his gaze hardens as it flicks over to me. "Just in case," he grumbles.

Miles disappears and Ainsley turns back to the hem of her shirt.

Well, ohhhhkay. Guess we've got some *family dynamics* to navigate here.

I spot some computer paper and help myself. Ainsley rolls a few colored pencils in my direction. Half an hour later—after her stomach starts making goblin noises—we're exploring the fridge and pantry, chatting about what we could make and laughing at how bad the fancy cheese in the cheese drawer smells.

Twice I think there's someone else standing there, but when I look up, we're alone. The third time, it's Reese in the doorway, smiling.

"I'm gonna head out in a minute," Reese says. "Do you wanna come help me pick my jewelry for the weekend, sweetie?"

Ainsley scampers after her mother and I'm left in the kitchen to make lunch. I put my hands on my hips and start a slow perusal of my options.

"How old are you?"

I jolt at the unexpected deep voice behind me. Miles is at the other end of the kitchen, leaning up against the counter.

"Twenty-eight. Are you staying for lunch?"

"I don't need you to feed me."

Good thing I'm not easily scared off. "Do you think Ainsley would want the white cheddar mac or the double-cheese stars and moons?"

"I think her mother would prefer she eats something that isn't pure chemicals."

I deftly ignore that, because Reese is presumably the person who bought the mac and cheese in the first place. I start searching through the cabinets for a pot. "How old are *you*?"

He frowns. "Got a lot of childcare experience?"

"Yes."

He's waiting for me to elaborate, but when I don't he crosses his arms over his chest. "What are you looking for?"

"A pot. There's a lot of real estate in this kitchen." I've opened six sets of doors and have yet to find the cookware.

He doesn't direct me toward it, which leads me to believe he either wants to make my life as hard as possible or he doesn't know his way around their kitchen.

Is *uncle* a euphemism? They don't seem to know each other very well. Or even *like* each other very well. Based on the way he's acting, I might have wondered if he was perhaps Ainsley's overprotective father, but Reese made it very clear when we spoke over the phone earlier in the week that she conceived Ainsley on her own and she's a single mother. Probably so I wouldn't put my foot in my mouth and ask Ainsley about her dad.

"Okey-doke," Reese says, reappearing with a rolling suitcase in one hand and Ainsley attached to the other. "I've gotta jet if I'm gonna make my flight." She bends and gives Ainsley a squeeze. "It's gonna be great. And it's only two nights. I'll see you after school on Monday."

Ainsley nods like they've already been over this. "I know."

"Okay. Well, Lenny, thank you. You're a lifesaver. Call me for *any* reason."

She gives Miles a nod and then heads to the front door. Ainsley trots after her and I migrate in that direction, wanting to give them some space for their goodbye but also wanting to be on hand.

Reese stops at the front door and slides her shoes on, saying something quietly to Ainsley.

"I *know,* Mom," Ainsley says, somewhat petulantly. "Just go already. You'll be late."

Reese gives her one last kiss on her staticky head and then the door clicks shut behind her.

Ainsley immediately power walks back in my direction, and even from here I can see that her eyes have gone watery and her chin is starting to quiver.

"What kind of movies do you like?" I ask her.

She skids to a stop. "I'm not allowed to watch movies during the day."

"Well, let's make an exception."

"Really?"

"Really."

"I like Indiana Jones."

I'm charmed. "Let's do it."

Ainsley happily eats two bowls of stars and moons while Indy punches his way through a crowd of fascists, and I consider that a win.

By the time we're done with lunch she doesn't seem so weepy anymore, but I want to keep her as distracted as possible, so we dig through the pantry and unearth a box of cake mix and frosting. We gleefully make a gigantic mess in the kitchen and I let her turn the vanilla frosting acid green with food coloring.

"You wanna know an old family tradition of mine?"

"Sure," she says, carefully mixing the frosting while her tongue is sticking out. She's wearing an apron fifty times too big and standing on one of the dining room chairs to reach the counter.

"When we make cupcakes, we always make one lucky one and hide it in with the rest."

"How do you make a lucky cupcake?"

"Well, first you fill the cups with batter, and then you pick one of them to be the lucky one. This one or this one?" I ask.

"That one." She points.

"Okay. And then you stick something unexpected into its batter."

"Like what?"

I open the fridge and consider my options. "Liiiike . . . ooh! Green olives. Or a little bit of lunch meat, maybe? How about—"

She bursts out laughing. "*Gross!*"

"Yes," I agree. "But so much fun. What should we choose?"

She scrambles down from the chair to come look. "How about those onions that Mom puts in fancy drinks?"

"Cocktail onions. PERFECT. I think you have a knack for this."

I open the jar for her and she pokes the onion so far into the cupcake she's got batter up to her third knuckle.

Her mom calls to check in while the cupcakes are baking and Ainsley starts to cry after they hang up. It seems like a good time to offer the little bit of videogame time she's allotted each day, and she jumps at the chance. By the time she's done zooming around the universe in a bright pink rocket ship, the cupcakes are cool enough to frost.

We each have a cupcake after dinner, and we decide we're both simultaneously relieved and disappointed to not get the lucky cupcake.

"It's getting late," Miles says from out of nowhere, and Ainsley and I both squeak and jump.

"Are you still here?!"

"It's her bedtime," he says, frowning and crossing his arms over his chest. I wouldn't say he's got a very gentle bedside manner, but I forgive him because he's wearing *that* sweatshirt and I'm in love and he's going to be my everything one day.

"Oh, you're right. Yeah. Things kind of got away from me."

"No kidding." He's frowning at the spilled batter on the counter, the dishes in the dripping sink, the opened packages of meat and cheese and bread I used to make sandwiches for dinner.

"I'll get to it," I say with a wave. I pull up Reese's email and refer to pages four and five. "Ainsley, shall we start the bedtime proceedings?"

She climbs down from the table and pads back toward her end of the apartment without a single complaint. Either she's tired or she doesn't know me well enough to argue yet.

She takes a shower and I help with the tricky buttons on her pajamas after she brushes her teeth. She E.T.'s herself into an impressively gigantic pile of stuffies and asks if she can read for a while before bed. I hand over her bedtime book, which is called *Squirrel Genius Mystery File #48,* and something tells me she's already read the other forty-seven.

"I'll be in the living room until Harper gets here to spend the night, but I'll see you bright and early, okay?"

She nods solemnly, already turning toward the wall with her book, and she just looks so tiny in her PJs. I let her have her privacy and gently click the door closed behind me.

The carpet in this place is a foot and a half thick so I pad soundlessly back toward the kitchen, freezing when I hear Miles hissing into his phone in the kitchen.

"Come on, Reese. She let Ainsley watch TV all day. They ate nothing but crap. Videogames for hours. The house is a total mess. Where did you even find this girl? . . . She looks like she's fresh off a week-and-a-half bender. Shouldn't we, I don't know, drug test her or something?"

And wow. Just like that. My love fantasy goes up in smoke.

What a total asshole.

I march into the kitchen and raise my eyebrows at him. He goes rigid, his eyes on mine, self-consciously running a hand over his hair. To my satisfaction he breaks eye contact first and leaves the room, finishing his phone call with Reese elsewhere.

In a flash I've got the kitchen polished to a high shine, so I gather my things and set up shop in the living room to wait for Harper.

I'm on the couch and digging through my backpack when:

"So—"

"Ah!" I jump at his sudden voice behind me. My backpack tumbles to the ground. "Quit doing that!"

"Sorry," he mumbles, and I can't tell which part he's apologizing for, but either way it's nowhere near enough. His eyes drop to my spilled backpack. My wallet and a book have skidded across the floor toward his feet. Our hands reach them at the same moment, but his freeze.

Grief and You, the title of the book blares up at us. *Life after the Death of a Loved One.*

I can feel his eyes flick from the book to my face and back.

I hate this book so much. If my mother hadn't given it to me at the funeral, inscribed with her sweet, perfect handwriting, I probably would have launched it into the Hudson River by now.

"So—" Oh, God. He's trying to talk again.

No. I've had enough for one night. I scramble the book into my bag.

"There are fresh-baked cupcakes in the kitchen," I offer sweetly, beating him to the punch and watching his face scrunch in confusion at my change in tone.

I turn away from him and flick on the TV. After a moment he seems to accept that there will be no more discussion from me and wordlessly heads back into the kitchen. I cross my fingers that he's selecting the cupcake at the top of the pyramid I engineered.

I strain toward the kitchen, turning the volume down just enough to hear him gag and cough. "What the fuck?" he mutters incredulously as he tosses the lucky cupcake in the trash.

I sigh with sweet, sweet satisfaction and settle back into the couch.

Two best friends sit facing one another on a twin bed. One of them will die too soon. The other one is me.

They are eating salt-and-vinegar potato chips and trying to figure out how life could possibly go on after unspeakable loss.

"Look . . . after this you're gonna have to come back to life at some point. You can't live dead, you know."

"Says who."

"Says me, your best friend."

"Fine then, Wise One. Lay it out for me. How. How am I supposed to come back to life after . . ."

"Oh, come on, complainer. Where's that happy-face T-shirt I bought you? You think that was ironic? No way. Life is for the living, yadda yadda."

"Easy for you to say, butthead. You're the one who won't have to go through all the after."

"OMG! I just came up with a brilliant idea for a T-shirt slogan. Ready?"

"Hit me."

"Life is what happens during the yadda yadda."

"We're going to be rich."

"Right?"

". . ."

". . ."

"You really have no idea how to live again on the other side of this? Like, seriously? No ideas?"

"Not one."

"Okay, fine. Here's what we'll do. We'll make it so easy. The easiest. We'll make it multiple choice."

"My life?"

"Yeah. We'll make a list. All you'll have to do is check the boxes. Pick task, perform task, reclaim your joie de vivre."

"A list for living again?"

"Bingo."

"Look, yes, you're my best friend. You obviously mean well. I know I'm not easy to be around sometimes. But . . . can we just not talk about this? Trying to imagine living again. Living without—Can we just not talk about this, please?"

"We're making the list. If you want to throw it in the garbage afterward, that's on you. Where's my pink pen?"

"I can't stop you, can I?"

"Item number one on the Live Again list: fall in love with a gorgeous man who is obsessed with you and is, like, a fireman or something."

"Wow, you even wrote the 'or something.' "

"There should be a little wiggle room to increase the odds of it actually happening."

" 'Kay. Got it. Gorgeous man. Should be easy."

"Atta girl. Item number two: wear ridiculously ugly clothes and pretend that they're expensive ugly, not cheap ugly. Then eat amuse bouche and go underbid on outrageously priced art."

"Unless 'amuse bouche' is a fancy word for 'chili dog,' I don't want it."

"Fine, just the art, then."

"The Met?"

"Always . . . I bet your mom would let you wear your grandma's vintage fur coats."

"Fine! But I want one of those little Jackie O hats where the lace comes down over your eyes."

"Deal. Wear whatever you want, the Met is on the list as its own bullet point. Now for the next item—"

"Can there be no more items for now? It hurts to think about it."

"I feel I should warn you. It's probably never going to not hurt. Just thought you should know."

"I know."

"And that's why you need the list. When I'm not around you can use it to—"

"Let's watch Clueless *and eat BLTs."*

"You're a true queen of distraction. Okay, fine, but only because you know bacon is my weak spot—Hey . . . You're not throwing the list in the trash?"

"Well. You're going through all this trouble to make it. I figure the least I can do is keep it safe."

This is a love story, I swear.

This is what happens when you've promised someone you'll live again.

Don’t miss Cara’s heartfelt
friends-to-lovers romance . . .

Available now from

HEADLINE
ETERNAL

Discover more charming rom-coms from Cara Bastone's Love Lines series

Could it be love
at first talk?

Is it love on the line?

Could this road trip lead
to romance?